CW00431310

OUR LADY OF

THE SERPENTS

BY THE SAME AUTHOR

Graffiti

OUR LADY OF
THE SERPENTS

Petrie Harbouri

BLOOMSBURY

First published 1999

Copyright © 1999 by Petrie Harbouri

The moral right of the author has been asserted

Bloomsbury Publishing Plc, 38 Soho Square, London W1V 5DF

A CIP catalogue record for this book
is available from the British Library

ISBN 0 7475 4332 1

10 9 8 7 6 5 4 3 2 1

Typeset by Palimpsest Book Production Limited,
Polmont, Stirlingshire
Printed by Clays Ltd, St Ives plc

ACKNOWLEDGMENTS

I am most grateful to Martin Gaethlich for
checking the reptile lore; any errors that
remain are entirely my own. I also owe special thanks to
Flavio Zanon who, without realising it,
suggested the garden to me.

I

Someone had once said that it was the hour when God walked in the garden. It was at any rate the time when everything begins to breathe again after the long hot hours in which life is suspended. Between the setting of the sun and the deepening of the twilight there is a brief moment when colours take on a strange resonance: the white flowers of the oleander are suddenly luminous, the straw colour of sere grasses stands out intensely, the browns and sepias and greys of tree trunks, branches and stones glow. Leaves which at noon were flat and one-dimensional now have a rich depth of greenness. It is as if all the bright light steadily absorbed throughout the day is being radiated back into the evening world. Then all too quickly these vibrations fade as light and colour drain from plants and rocks and walls; overhead the first faint stars can be seen, though the horizon still shades into pale turquoise. The giving out has become a gathering in, a pause before the life of darkness sets in. It was the time of day, she told him, when she usually walked a little in the garden.

'Come and see it before it gets quite dark,' she said and escorted him down the four broad stone steps from the terrace, their balustrade still warm to the touch. ('The lizard steps' she called them, but Robert, feeling his way, wondering whether all this was perhaps not such a good idea, neither heeded this name nor questioned it.) When the house was in its heyday this would have been the hour at which servants started folding back the wooden shutters that had been tightly closed all day against the sun, carried cool drinks out on to the terrace on silver trays . . . These days though the paint was peeling off the shutters and most of them remained permanently fastened.

'It is a large house for just myself,' she had told him over the telephone. 'We can have a drink on the terrace,' she said now, 'but I'd like you to see the garden a bit first.' Then, as if making polite conversation, 'This is an old garden, you know' (pointing to knotted trunks thicker than two hands could span) 'those bougainvilleas were planted nearly a hundred years ago. They do rather need some attention, their weight is pulling the pergola down.' And added, 'I can no longer tackle them.'

Looking at her thin brown forearms and fragile wrists, Robert could see why. Ringless fingers, small bony claws with pale unvarnished nails cut short, rested lightly on his own arm for a moment as they turned back towards the house.

'Should have done it years ago, but never mind.'

'She is something of a recluse,' Anthony had said. 'A slight reputation for eccentricity, keeps the gate padlocked, a lot of people would love to see the house and garden but she rarely lets anyone in, been living alone there for years. You hear some odd things about her locally – I have a vague idea there was once some dramatic piece of gossip or scandal – yet people seem to respect her all the same. She's a bit of a *grande dame* perhaps but it might suit you.'

Chloe had replied promptly to Robert's letter, cool and brisk. 'I cannot offer very much in the way of salary, if that is what you are wanting,' she declared firmly in confident black ink. 'I can offer you bed and board, peace and quiet, hard work and half the amount that I pay my housekeeper. I could not possibly give you the same amount or she would be deeply hurt and jealous.'

*   *   *

The housekeeper did not appear to be overtly hostile, even if somewhat dour: black-clad and silent, she brought out a battered silver tray with a decanter of wine and glasses. Robert fell back on the sort of placating smile and too profuse thank-yous that are commonly used with other people's unknown servants or strangers whose language you don't speak; the lack of any smile in response made him feel at the same time uncomfortable and annoyed with himself for this discomfort.

'She's suspending judgment on you,' explained Chloe a few days later. 'I sacked your predecessor, you know, and Maria's waiting to see if you'll go the same way.'

Robert, suddenly sensitive to cross-currents of feeling, wondered whether Maria might not perhaps have had some other candidate lined up for the job.

'Clever of you,' she said when he voiced this thought, 'yes, as far as the garden is concerned she had various lads from the village in mind. If you decide you want to stay and I decide I like you, we may very well call on one of them in due course to come and help with some of the heaviest work.'

'I think I should tell you,' he had said that first evening, 'that I am not really a gardener. I would not want you to have any illusions. I like plants, I like trying to make things grow, but I have no special training or anything.'

'I'm not sure that a gardener is quite what I want' (she smiled faintly) 'not even the harmless sort in a grubby vest and a battered straw hat. I certainly wouldn't want someone who would prune and trim and cut back and try to impose on this garden. This is where Maria and I differ. She thinks that the garden is a disgraceful jungle and that I need someone to deal with it. What I want is a man about the house, someone who will take care of the garden, come to the dinner table with clean fingernails and provide me with a modicum of civilised conversation. A sort of *sieur de compagnie* if that is the male equivalent of the kind of respectable person who keeps company to elderly ladies.'

As a job description this left rather a lot unclarified. Robert sipped his wine and felt unsure. By now night had fallen. On the faded wall of the house fat pinkish-beige geckos of various sizes had come out to hunt the moths drawn by the lamp. Beyond the circle of its light the garden was dark, still save for an occasional mysterious rustle, quiet save for the trilling of crickets. From time to time the geckos chittered and squeaked. Chloe did not apparently feel the need to say anything further. And it was probably her silence, the strangeness of everything, some sense of tranquillity that made Robert agree to a trial month in spite of himself.

'I don't want neatness,' she said as he started work in the garden, 'I like it the way it is, I simply want it to be cared for. Minimal tidiness, yes all right, paths and hedges – but really what I need is someone who will appreciate the spirit of the place. And do precisely what I say.' She smiled as if to take the sting out of the words. 'I expect to be obeyed. There are two rules in this garden: nothing is to be done unless I say so, and nothing, nothing at all, is ever to be killed. If you have a problem with either of these things you'd better say so now' (sharp tone reminding Robert he was on probation).

'What do you think about it? How does she seem?' asked Anthony when they met for a drink after Robert had been at the Villa for a week. 'Not sure,' was Robert's reply, but he was increasingly beginning to think that he could manage to work for Chloe (whether she would consider that he measured up to her standards being another matter: Robert possessed a nail-brush but feared that he had never been much of a conversationalist. 'You don't have to apologise for existing,' Annie had once snapped at him).

He began weeding and raking the gravel paths nearest the house. They were more baked earth than gravel. 'It's getting a bit thin,' he suggested tentatively one morning when Chloe came down into the garden to check on work in progress, 'if you wanted to get in a load of new gravel I could spread it for you and it might stay weed-free longer.'

'Yes, we could perhaps do that. I'll think about it,' she replied.

Robert wondered whether that 'we' might betoken some acceptance, although his trial month was not yet up.

Chloe said, 'Wait, there's a spider in your hair, bend down.' He bent obediently, she caught the spider carefully in her two cupped hands, then shook it gently out at a safe distance from his rake. 'I like carefulness,' she said, and sat down on the steps. 'What do people call you?' she asked a few minutes later.

'Just plain Robert,' he replied and went on working.

She watched for a while. Then, 'I got rid of the German – your predecessor – because he proved to be quite unacceptable,' she continued. 'I thought he might do because he played the piano, but it was an error of judgment on my part, he wouldn't do at all. He offended three times so he had to go. Do you play the piano, by the way? I didn't ask.'

'No,' said Robert, 'I'm afraid I don't.' Not much liking the apologetic tone of this, he added, on what he hoped was a firmer note, 'If you told me what he did that was so objectionable, I could perhaps avoid the same offences.'

'Ah,' she said, 'well yes, perhaps . . . I'll tell you the two lesser crimes anyway. To begin with, he urinated on the box hedges.' (This was not at all what Robert had been expecting.) 'Now of course I don't mind if you have the odd pee in the garden, but the compost heap would be a better place, or the bare earth if you must, *not* the box hedges. It scorches them if you do it repeatedly.'

'And the second thing?'

'The second thing,' said Chloe. 'was sex.' She frowned. Robert made polite noises of the 'Oh dear, I see' kind. She continued: 'He had a rather crude encounter in the garden with a girl from the village. Six of one and half a dozen of the other I dare say, doubtless she'd been hanging round making eyes at him, very unlikely he was the first, but all the same I did not like it – he pulled her skirt up and her knickers down, pushed her forwards over the parapet of the cistern till the wretched girl's face was almost in the water and, well, let's not mince words, fucked her rather definitively.'

This description was even less what Robert had been expecting; he felt more than a little uncomfortable. She noted his expression.

'You don't find my choice of language very ladylike, do you? As a matter of fact I can think of several much cruder terms to describe that act but I thought I'd spare your blushes. And one may as well be accurate. By the way, if you're wondering how I happened to see them, the answer is binoculars, and though perhaps *you* may be the kind of decent person who would have averted his eyes as soon as he spotted what was going on *I* am definitely not, I watched from beginning to end, though I must say from beginning to end did not take more than a couple of minutes. As far as I could see there wasn't a single word spoken. I did not like it at all. The whole thing had a sort of abruptness and brutality about it which was horribly wrong.' A sudden brief wash of emotion clouded her face; Robert half-registered it as sadness. 'I've embarrassed you. Forgive me. But perhaps this is an opportunity to say something a tiny bit impertinent – your private life is of course entirely your own business but do please keep clear

of the village. Get a taxi into town if you feel libidinous.'
Robert cleared his throat in even more acute embarrassment.
She got up. 'I'll leave you now to get on with the gravel.' She
looked frail and tired. 'Lunch in three-quarters of an hour.'

Robert felt slightly daunted at the thought of further conversations of this kind. At the lunch table, however, they
spoke mostly of the Common Agricultural Policy and its
effects on traditional farming; 'Such a mistake to uproot all
those centuries-old olive trees,' she declared.

*'They were planted generations ago,' she had said, 'they're
more like trees now, my hands don't meet around them,' yet
the four hands spanning the knotted and curving trunk of
the bougainvillea met, two larger hands, pale and ringless,
two smaller and brown, a black pearl on one finger, a plain
gold band on another. And this was how it began perhaps:
hands meeting on rough bark, fingers delicately brushing,
tentatively as if by mistake, then once more, not by mistake,
eyes meeting, nothing said, the sap surging and coursing in a
sympathetic jolt through the old gnarled wood. The morning
is a businesslike time to visit the garden; the cool of the
evening, just before dusk, is the romantic time – to wander
beneath the trees, maybe to show it off to guests; but in the
burning midsummer noon hours the garden is usually left to
itself. For this is the dead time, the dangerous time, the silent
time, the passionate time: the haunting time perhaps when the
joins – usually seamless – between this and other worlds strain
and shudder for an instant. It is also the primitive time, the
hour when small reptiles and insects once more rule the earth
as birds and mammals retire to the shade to rest. The silent
time is full of noise: the cicadas are remorseless – yet this is
not a contradiction, for their repetitive, rhythmic, deafening
rasping serves only to emphasise the essential quiet. Under
the bougainvillea arbour the shade lies deep and still. In the*

bright light below, on the stone terracing, an emerald-green lizard basks, sunning itself, motionless save for the faintest pulse in its throat. She points it out to him. 'You have petals in your hair,' he says and puts out his hand to pick off the papery magenta and crimson bracts, one by one. He places them carefully in the pocket of his shirt. A faint pulse beats in his throat. The smell of his sweat: sharp and green and urgent.

'Your predecessor was screwing her morning, noon and night – or so they say. He was youngish, one of those rather camp-looking Germans, all cropped blond hair and steely blue eyes and sadistic black leather boots, well, metaphorical boots anyway if you know what I mean, I seem to remember that he actually wore expensive trainers most of the time. He played Chopin soulfully by candlelight when he wasn't hard at work between her sheets. No one seems quite sure whether she threw him out because she didn't fancy some of his more recherché tastes or whether it was the other way round, that she sucked him dry and spat out the pips, and he slunk off exhausted when he could no longer rise, as it were, to her demands.'

'I don't believe a word of it.'

'No, neither do I as a matter of fact.' (Delighted laugh.) 'But I told you there were stories about her, and that's one of them.'

'For God's sake, Anthony, she's old, she must be over eighty . . .' (Robert was shocked.) 'I don't think you ought to go round repeating that sort of gossip.'

'Come on, I like gossip. And I'm not broadcasting it, I'm telling it to you. I didn't tell you earlier because I thought it might scare you off . . . Anyway, if you were a blameless eighty-year-old and word got about that you were ardently dallying with some sexy little blonde, you'd probably feel rather pleased and proud, wouldn't you?'

'It's not the same,' maintained Robert, but couldn't explain why.

'Write it all down, write about it,' someone else had said (one of the kindly, blundering, insensitive busybodies), as if this was an easy matter, a cheap and simple remedy for everything from broken hearts to broken lives. Chloe had no desire to write about it, either then or later. What came to fill her notebooks in the silent evening hours was something slightly different.

Thus: 'The cistern,' she wrote, 'was originally used for watering the garden. In those days people had to rely entirely on rain water collected during the winter, which is why all the early planting in this garden – the trees and the box hedges and the bougainvilleas of course – were things which did not need more than the occasional soak. It was a mark of genius on the part of the original designer of the garden to see that the cistern could be not only functional but also ornamental – cisterns of this date are usually large, rectangular, covered utilitarian structures, whereas here it was clearly conceived of as being a central feature: it is thus square, effectively forming a raised pond surrounded by a waist-high stone parapet. Such an arrangement would, of course, lead to various problems, such as infestation by mosquitoes and – more seriously – loss of water through evaporation. The first of these problems was solved by keeping fish in the cistern; the second could not be solved, and probably explains why at some later date an additional closed cistern of the more usual type was added, with a removable cover so that rain could be collected in winter and evaporation prevented in summer. Occasionally eels were placed in such cisterns to keep the water sweet, though I have no means of knowing whether this was done here. Water for the house came from the well, and was also used sparingly.

'After mains-water was brought to the area, the feel of the garden changed as more flowering shrubs were planted; an increasingly wide range of garden plants was gradually becoming available and it is probable that most of the hibiscuses date from this second phase. It was now too that the irrigation channels which meander through the garden were disconnected from the cistern and the lotuses were planted in it to complete its transformation into a pond.'

Lying forward over the cistern with your face above the water. 'If you keep still,' he says, 'you will see your reflection among the lotuses.' 'I cannot keep still,' she says, 'unless you do.'

'These days,' said Chloe, 'metred water is rather expensive, which is why I've gradually been reducing the watered bits of the garden and letting more of it run wild and dry. I do not wish the cistern to be used for irrigation,' she added sharply, as if forestalling a suggestion that Robert might have voiced, 'I like it the way it is with the fish and the lotuses.'

'Robert is such a *wimp*,' Annie had once said to herself in exasperation. And to him, 'Why don't you ever stand up for yourself, why don't you disagree if you think I'm wrong?' Or, on another occasion, 'Oh God, why can't you be more *masterful*?' Such exasperation rarely achieves the desired effect, as Annie herself was all too well aware. Now: 'I am her servant,' Robert might have written to Annie (but didn't). And what he might have meant is that in the employer-servant relationship there exists the possibility of abdicating all responsibility, of subsuming self: this is perhaps why Robert found Chloe restful.

For there is no doubt that an imposed discipline (military perhaps, or monastic) simplifies life: choices – the very act of choosing – can be painful. 'Annie, I think I shan't come back at once,' was what Robert had finally managed to write. 'Perhaps it might be better for both of us to let things rest a bit. I'll try to find work of some kind here for a few months. Anthony has heard of someone who wants a live-in gardener – which sounds as if it might be a possibility. I'll let you know as soon as I fix something.' And had added as a sad, scrawled postscript, 'I'm sorry.'

Pace the gossip-mongers, small, frail, white-haired Chloe as dominatrix is rather a far-fetched image. Moreover, servants rarely sit down to dinner with their mistresses. Yet some abdication of responsibility was probably involved; certainly life with Chloe was circumscribed within orderly limits that were comfortable to Robert: up at dawn, watering before the sun rose too high in the sky, work in the garden followed by lunch in the relative cool of the dim, old-fashioned dining-room, a siesta, the afternoon to himself (plenty of time for drawing), and finally – after a shower and a change into a clean, freshly pressed shirt – dinner on the terrace. Her swift, sure pronouncements on garden matters were soothing rather than irritating: 'No,' she said, 'I do not wish you to prune the orange hibiscus, or to attempt to propagate it either. Not at all a good idea. It's a great mistake to want to have too much of a good thing. I want there to be just the single one, and I want it to grow freely as large as it likes.' Robert obeyed.

Night falls early in the Mediterranean summer. As they sat on the terrace Robert was intrigued by the geckos. 'They're said to bring good luck to a house,' Chloe told him.

'They do seem rather aggressive sometimes though,' he noted, watching them chase each other. 'And greedy.' (The moths drawn by the luring lamp were promptly disposed of as they settled for a fatal moment on the wall.) 'I've always been fascinated by the speed with which lizards catch and swallow their prey.'

'Do you like lizards?' (Not such a curious question to ask in the circumstances perhaps.)

'Yes, I do rather. When I was about ten or eleven I kept a green lizard as a pet for a while. I got very adept at catching flies to feed it with.'

'*Lacerta viridis*, or was it *trilineata*?'

'*Viridis*.' (He smiled.) 'So you like lizards, too.'

She did not answer the implied question, merely telling him in a manner that was suddenly formally conversational, 'There is supposed still to be a small population of chameleons on this island. They're very rare though, I've only ever seen one once – and that was many, many years ago.'

Some coolness in her voice made Robert feel that the subject of lizards was to be dropped. He thus replied in equally neutral tones, 'Well, I'll certainly keep my eyes open then.'

Maria served dinner. Chloe talked competently and fluently about local beliefs and superstitions, the lucky and the unlucky ('It is considered extremely unwise, if not downright dangerous, to go to sleep in the shade of a fig tree,' for example.) In spite of the fluency, Robert thought that there was an undertone of distraction, as if her mind was elsewhere. However, when they had finished eating and were sitting sipping their tiny cups of hot, thick, dark coffee, she appeared to relax and said, 'If you turn off the light we should be able to see the Milky Way. That's one of the great advantages of not living too near a town.' Robert obeyed. They sat in silence gazing at the broad swathe of light stretching across the night sky. The trilling crickets, the occasional plaintive call of a scops owl, the blackness of the cypresses.

The cypress trees stand dark and silent in the quivering midday heat. 'I want, I want, I want,' she says, 'I want more and more, I want too much of a good thing,' and she arches her back against the aged trunk of the cypress tree. 'This is your tree,' she tells him, 'sempervirens should be semper vir, *a tree tall and erect, sensitive to each faintest breath of God's will . . .' But, 'Ah,' he answers, 'you will have to wait, I am afraid, your humblest of servants is only human.' After a while, 'I am your servant,' he murmurs as he kneels before her with his face pressed close between her thighs.*

2

Robert dreamed that he had lost his lizard. He was tossing and turning, feverish, restless, in his new school pyjamas – for some illness seemed to have kept him at home long after term had begun – and was tormented by the knowledge that the lizard had escaped. Moonlight poured into his room. He got up, knowing that he must search for it, knowing that catastrophe could only be averted if he found it. Curiously, as he tiptoed downstairs and into the garden, the moonlight changed to become the dim aquamarine light of the end of a long northern summer evening. Everything in the garden seemed intensified, the apple tree was formidable, total silence made itself felt. Robert's anxiety increased. Suddenly he saw the lizard on the wall at the bottom of their suburban garden. It seemed to have tripled in size. It gave off an unearthly greenish glow, like a glow-worm. Robert felt both great reverence and a powerful driving desire to possess it. He reached out his hand. The lizard made no movement beyond the slight throbbing of a pulse in its throat. It looked at him. He knew he would never possess it.

Robert woke in the early hours to find his pillow damp, was puzzled until he realised he must have been crying. He parted the mosquito net, got up, had a drink of water, then stood at the window looking at the stars and listening to the sounds of the night. He felt alien and lonely and discouraged.

*   *   *

'Darling Annie,' he wrote a few days later, 'I miss you terribly.'
He then tore off the sheet of paper, crumpled it up into a ball
and aimed it across the room at the waste-paper basket. It
fell short. He sighed, went and picked it up, smoothed it out,
reread the few words, then threw it away again. He lay down
on his narrow bed in the half-light of the shuttered room. The
solitary hot afternoon hours.

'Look at it this way,' said Anthony, 'the fact that one has
done something, made a decision, usually means that it was
the right thing to do.'

Robert felt that there was a fault in this argument somewhere, but couldn't pinpoint it. 'I miss Annie, I can't help
wondering if I've done the wrong thing . . .' he had finally
admitted when pressed by Anthony to account for his general
air of gloomy restlessness during the humid, heavy August
days. ('Is Madame Chloe proving too demanding a mistress?' 'No, of course not, stop being so incredibly, *pruriently*
stupid . . .')

Anthony was rarely stupid, although he had frequently
offended Robert during the long years of their friendship.
Thus, musing: 'Of course, there are always whores, you
know.' (No response.) 'In this town the market seems to
have been cornered by Russians and Bulgarians – the local
talent is more semi-professional if you know what I mean –
but a competent, sturdy Slavic lady might be some kind of
answer, do you think? Or no, on second thoughts perhaps not
quite your cup of tea,' he concluded hastily, seeing Robert's
expression.

'No,' said Robert shortly.

As it happened, Robert had already encountered one of
the Russian girls and his response had been an embarrassed
'No'. After Chloe discovered that he possessed a clean driving
licence and decided that he could be trusted, she had taken

Robert over to one of the outbuildings and shown him an elderly, rather dusty car. 'I imagine it still works,' she said, 'though I haven't driven it for more than a year.' Thus Robert was no longer dependent on the infrequent local bus service or on taxis when he wanted to visit the town; indeed, he was occasionally entrusted with small errands. ('You've made a hit,' commented Anthony, 'she never let that strapping young Prussian in his jackboots anywhere near her car.') And thus it was that Robert went early one Saturday morning to the weekly market and as he made his way back to the alley in which he'd parked the car was accosted by the Russian. Her words were in a language that Robert didn't understand: their meaning perfectly comprehensible. And, 'No,' Robert stammered awkwardly in English. 'No thank you, no' (or something of this kind) and hurried to the car, feeling her eyes on his back. For a moment he feared that it wasn't going to start, then crashed the gears clumsily; as he manoeuvred through the town traffic he thought to himself that eight o'clock in the morning was a rather strange time for her to be at work, then – on quiet country roads by now – supposed that a market is after all a good place for business of all kinds.

She is a wordless lover on the whole, feeling no need for murmured endearments, yet once in a moment of abandon cries, 'You have found me.' He asks her about it later as they prepare to part (brushing off the dust, picking twigs and leaves from her hair, smoothing out crumpled garments, retrieving a sandal cast heedlessly aside). 'You seek and you quest and you find me,' is all she will say. He likes the fact that when found her eyes are wide open.

One of the strangenesses at first, one of the things that shocked Robert in some obscure way, was the colour in Chloe's garden. Crimson, scarlet, vermilion, magenta, orange:

insistent, uncompromising, blazing colours that stare at you with insolent confidence. Colours belonging to plants that sprawl, that lounge, that strut, that tangle in rampant profusion. Gradually though, as the weeks passed, he began to feel somehow more comfortable with these unequivocal colours and to understand Chloe's rule about the sparing use of secateurs. For the shocking is in some way seductive; this, it says, is a different world – and it beckons you to enter it.

Lunch was a meal that properly belonged in a more restrained and familiar context of polished dining-table and matching chairs, of white napkins, long-instilled manners, of the discreet chinking of knives and forks on china plates. There are thoughts that never surface, that never reach the level of words; thus, 'It is women who instil manners into the male child,' was Robert's not-quite-thought: 'Don't scrape your spoon, keep your elbows in, sit up straight, don't slouch, don't talk with your mouth full.' (Prohibitions mostly.) Dinner on the terrace was more relaxed. Robert felt that less was expected of him in the way of conversation (though why this should be so he would have been unable to explain). After they had eaten, Chloe liked to turn off the lamp and sit in the darkness looking at the stars. She usually smoked a cigar with her coffee and was frequently rather silent. Such evening silences were not uncomfortable; on the contrary, they offered easy spaces in which to think aloud.

'One of the reasons why people feel less sympathy for reptiles than for mammals,' she mused, 'is the fact that they have no obvious ears. Which of course makes it less easy to have the sort of safe, unthinking sense of kinship that one has for cats or dogs or horses. I think in some it might be the lack of eyelids too,' she added. 'After all, a face with two ears, two eyes and a mouth is familiar, but a face with a mouth to bite you, two unblinking eyes to gaze at you and no ears to listen as you beg and plead is definitely frightening.'

Robert considered this idea. 'Perhaps one feels – rightly or wrongly – that one can communicate with mammals, whereas with reptiles there's no such possibility,' he offered. 'Actually, what I always used to like best about the lizard I kept as a child was its hands.'

She laughed. 'Maybe,' she said, 'you have just explained exactly why people like snakes even less than they like lizards.'

'Upon thy belly shalt thou go,' pronounced God, as if this was a curse or humiliation.

'Look,' he calls quietly, 'I want to show you something.' He is squatting under the loquat tree. He has caught a skink, which at first sight seems to her like a short, plump, striped snake. He points out its legs, tiny and rudimentary. 'Even the legless lizards had legs not so very long ago,' he tells her. (His time-scale is slightly different from most people's.) 'If you dissected a slow-worm – well, or if you X-rayed it, of course – you'd see that it still has vestigial leg bones.' He lets the skink go and stands up. His hands are almost as brown as hers now, square, confident hands, delicate hands capable of feeling and finding, of dissecting a lizard.

'Word has it,' said Anthony, 'that she keeps a mad husband locked up in the attic. Rather Brontëish.'

'There aren't any attics,' stated Robert flatly, 'only a cellar, and all that it has in it is wine and olive-oil and potatoes and such like.'

'Robert, you are prosaic as well as being literal-minded,' was Anthony's rebuke. Then a smile. 'Actually,' he said, 'it's a lot more likely that he's buried in the garden. She buried *someone* there anyway, though the other version claims it was her lover, not her husband.'

*   *   *

Chloe had written: 'Gardens in hot climates are not tame places. Tranquil expanses of greensward and quiet colours are as alien to this land as gentle Jesus meek and mild is to Jehovah, the jealous God.' The thought of Jehovah somehow did not please her. She continued: 'The god of these gardens is Dionysos, lord of profusion and growth and ecstasy, untrammelled and prodigal. A great mistake to imagine that he is the god of wine – a foolish, drunken, bleary-eyed Bacchus: he is the god of the vine, of passionate and cruel green growth that knows no boundaries or measure. His eyes are open wide, unblinking, unseeing, uncaring.'

As she sat at the window in the late, late hours her pen drew curlicues in the margin, which became convoluted tendrils and then turned into a profuse and prodigal grape-laden vine, growing till it encompassed the text. She thought of the epicene, feminised, ambisexual body with which Dionysos is usually represented, thought too of Jesus with his spaniel eyes and flowing locks and of the curious *void* that exists beneath his carefully draped loincloth as he hangs on the cross, that absence of any sex. She sighed. For a moment she considered tearing out this page, yet somehow liked her vine; thus she merely sighed once more, turned over the page and started again. 'What makes the brilliance of scarlet hibiscuses, orange campsis, magenta bougainvillea so beautiful and satisfying is their luminosity,' she wrote. 'The same colours printed on cloth or paper would be flat and merely garish, but the petals of flowers are lambent, impregnated with light.'

There did not seem much else to say, so Chloe gave up, closed her exercise book and went to bed. For a long time she lay on her back in wakefulness, but finally turned to one side and slept.

'Bell flowers are reticent,' she says, 'but trumpet flowers flaunt their invitation to the fumbling bees.' The hibiscus flares and

flaunts, vibrant orange shading in its depths to shocking pink, the protruding style tipped with vermilion. 'It is the most erotic flower I have ever seen,' *he says.*

Tongues exploring the body's secret folds: inner elbow, armpit, buttocks, groin. The taste of the sweat lying in the crease beneath her breasts. The different textures of his hair from nape to underarm to pubis. The taste of his semen: sharp and sudden and salty-sweet.

'What I cannot stand is pussy-footing politeness in gardens,' pronounced Chloe, 'I like plants that have the courage of their convictions.'

Robert thought of Annie's subtle dusky pinks and quiet mauves and silvers, punctuated with an occasional discreet touch of the palest of sulphur yellows, and was flooded with a surge of tenderness. 'Politeness is not a bad quality,' he replied after a moment, in obscure defence of a great amorphous swirl of memory and nostalgia.

'No, indeed.'

Chloe was sitting on a bench in the shade eating sunflower seeds, cracking them between her teeth and spitting out the husks; Robert, wearing an ancient, battered linen hat with a floppy brim that she had found for him from out of the depths of some chest or wardrobe, was clipping one of the (now unscorched) box hedges a few feet away from her. The dusty, peppery, pleasant smell of box, familiar and comfortable. She smiled. 'You have to admit though, it's the enemy of passion.'

The rhythmic sound of the shears. For 'passion' is one of those words like 'religion' which – even if not exactly taboo – often give rise to a certain awkwardness or uneasiness when they crop up in conversation between relative strangers. Perhaps it is simply that they refer to such subjective experiences that there is not much room for discussion. (Like colours maybe – it is hard to imagine a conversation about viridian, for example, or ultramarine.) And thus Robert made no response other than a noncommittal grunt and went on with his clipping.

Chloe cracked her sunflower seeds for a minute or two, then said, 'Next spring, God willing, I'll show you the most impolite plant in the whole garden.'

It occurred to Robert that she might be teasing him.

One of the advantages – or disadvantages – of a small town is that you tend to run into people. Robert had now come across the Russian girl two more times (though perhaps this is not really so surprising: for another thing about small towns is that parking can be a problem – and even more so when the place is overrun by tourists – so that he generally left Chloe's car in the same narrow alley near the market area and continued on foot). On the first of these encounters Robert simply crossed the road and went on his way at a slightly faster pace; on the second their eyes met and he felt a little ashamed of himself. 'I could at least be polite,' he thought – and thus said, 'Good afternoon,' to which she replied with what sounded like an ordinary greeting.

He was smiling as he rang Anthony's bell.

'You're looking remarkably cheerful for a change. Anything you can share? Do tell.'

'Oh, nothing special, just various thoughts about passion and politeness.'

'Polite passion or passionate politeness? It doesn't sound to me like a very good mixture,' said Anthony doubtfully.

Robert wrote to Annie quite often. Since passion is not the only emotion whose dimensions are too unwieldy to be easily expressed in words, large parts of these letters were taken up by descriptions: of Chloe, of her house, of her garden. 'You'd like it, Annie,' he told her. 'It's full of extraordinary flowering shrubs, half of which I don't recognise – though you'd probably know what they are. I'm a bit shy about revealing the extent of my ignorance to Chloe by asking.' And in another letter: 'It's not a garden of vistas, but a rather intensely *inward-turning place*' (underlined twice). 'In fact the main part of the garden is enclosed within massive stone walls which Chloe says are as old as the oldest part of the house. They lean out of true and bulge perilously in places, but at some point have been shored up from the outside with great buttresses which now look almost as if they grew organically from the walls. Inside they're covered with all sorts of climbing plants growing in great tangled ropes – I don't know if the wall supports the plants or if by now it's the plants that are supporting the wall.'

A garden of vistas is quite clearly a garden for viewing. The purpose of a labyrinthine jungle turned in upon itself is less obvious – though this was not something that Robert thought about. (The paths that meandered through it, emerging suddenly on the open space with the six tall palm trees and the cistern, might suggest that it was meant to be walked in. By whom though and when?) Robert was not entirely sure how much of the garden was visible through the trees from the various rooms of the house. He had not forgotten Chloe's binoculars; the sense of being watched is uneasy – even if all one is doing is blameless weeding.

It is easiest to meet in the long, hot hours when everyone else is asleep. Once, though, she finds him by the cistern in the magic expectant time just before dusk. The swifts are swooping low over the water as they hunt mosquitoes in the evening cool. 'I love this time of day,' he tells her, 'it is the hour when God

walked in the garden.' 'But he was so jealous and punitive,'
she says sadly. He kisses her: a brief, tender brushing of lips.
'Tomorrow,' he says. The first bats are beginning to emerge.

Summer evenings are full of expectancy and promise. As the
light fades there is a quickening of hope; tired, sweaty bodies
are showered, limp weary clothes discarded and replaced with
something fresh, the day's stubble is perhaps shaved. Eau-de-
Cologne and high-heeled sandals clicking over the polished
wood of the bedroom floor (for the rugs have long since
been cleaned and put away with mothballs for the summer).
Perhaps you sally forth in search of whatever adventure the
night may bring (if you are young and fancy-free); perhaps
you anticipate friends around the table under the stars, the
pleasures of relaxed conversation and good food. Perhaps the
clean shirt or the scent and the earrings and the sandals are
rituals for yourself alone. But hope is a primitive, irrepressible
response to the falling of darkness in summer.

'I like rituals,' said Chloe, 'and this is why there are fixed times
for meals.'
   'Sorry.' Robert had been up to the village to post some
letters, had sat under the ancient plane tree having a drink,
unconsciously savouring the promise in the air, watching and
listening to the life around him, and then had noticed the time
and hurried back, to emerge on the terrace ten minutes later
than usual. 'I do apologise. I was in the village.'
   'If you were in the village then you must have been watching
the evening *volta*, that little promenade when the boys and the
girls come out in twos and threes and stroll up and down the
main street or round the square . . . It's a sort of ritual mating
game actually, covert glances, watching and being watched,
nothing said, just a few giggles from time to time on one side
and the occasional self-conscious guffaw on the other.'

Chloe poured wine for both of them. Robert had noticed on the very first evening that round the narrow neck of the decanter was what appeared to be a gold ring set with a solitaire diamond; uncertain of himself in Chloe's world, he had thought it more diplomatic to make no comment. The diamond now flashed in the lamplight as she filled his glass.

'Yes, I noticed,' he said. 'Everyone seems so severely segregated though, the boys and girls parading up and down separately, the men in the coffee house, the old women sitting gossiping at their doorsteps . . .' He laughed. 'I hadn't realised until a few days ago what those whitewashed stones outside the threshold were for.'

'"Grandmother stones" we used to call them,' she said, 'though some people bring out chairs these days.'

Life lived in public. Watching and being watched: no uneasiness here unless it is felt by the stranger who does not belong and who watches the watchers from an alien distance.

'As a matter of fact,' said Chloe, 'appearances can be deceptive and things are changing far more rapidly than you might think. It's a question of altered expectations. An awful lot seems to be written these days about the effects of mass tourism on the environment, yet as far as I know no one has produced a doctoral thesis on the way it affects the sex life of village boys. These days the more confident and those with a bit of cash in their pockets set off for the bright lights of town – extremely dark and noisy discotheques actually – in the hope of finding some skimpily clad tourist girl who won't say no to a romantic walk along the beach or a brief grope and fumble under the old walls or whatever, and those who can't quite manage to *score* (I think that's the right word, isn't it?) at any rate have their hopes and expectations and envies aroused.' Chloe laughed. 'Incidentally, that's the main reason why they're all so keen to learn English. Older women are also sometimes rather a good bet,' she added, 'or older men too if they've got a bit of money, though no one ever admits this. Not shocking you, am I?'

'Not in the least,' said Robert, who by now felt able to take some of Chloe's more improbable topics of conversation in his stride. (If he had coloured faintly, this was for a different reason; his back was to the light, however, and it is to be doubted that Chloe had noticed his slight blush.)

'Poor things, it makes a change from the ewes, anyway.' (This did shock Robert.)

'You should hear them swapping stories,' Chloe continued, just as he was wondering where her information came from. 'People tend to forget that voices carry and that open windows can be listened from, though I must say I can't help thinking that the lads working here last week were a pair of terrible liars.'

(The six stately palm trees around the cistern had been burdened with many years' worth of dead fronds. 'It means ropes and climbing, I rather think,' Chloe declared; Robert had answered firmly, 'I don't have a very good head for heights, I'm afraid,' at which she'd laughed and said, 'Goodness, of course not, I wouldn't dream of asking you to climb trees, we'll get a couple of boys from the village to do it.' They had seemed pleasant enough young men, with curly dark hair, strong muscular thighs and arms and an equally powerful smell of sweat and tobacco; it had not occurred to Robert to wonder about the content of their cheerful banter as they set about barbering the palm trees.)

'Anyway,' Chloe concluded, 'regardless of those poor boys' boasting, the fact is that things are changing – which is why quite a few of the girls nowadays are also no better than they should be.' (It was a long time since Robert had heard this expression used.)

*　　*　　*

Robert himself, forty years old, diffident, tall and thin, with light-brown hair (also getting a bit thin, let it be said), a prominent Adam's apple and an unmemorable face, was not an obvious candidate for the role of Mediterranean lover. And yet . . .

. . . And yet – to use Anthony's expression – everyone is *someone's* cup of tea (well, almost everyone), there's no accounting for tastes, and Robert at any rate presented an unthreatening image. According to his agreement with Chloe, Saturday nights were his own; he tended to go into town and often ate at a restaurant on the port where the fact that he was beginning to be greeted as a regular customer among the hordes of anonymous tourists was in some small way gratifying. He usually had a book with him and sometimes read, though more often simply watched the toings and froings along the waterfront. And one night got into conversation with the two Dutch women sitting at the table next to his. They were primary school teachers, they told him, and he was what? A freelance illustrator of children's books? (Robert preferred not to say 'a gardener' or 'an old lady's companion'.) How very interesting, and what a *big* responsibility, the forming of the visual imagination in the young . . . They were pleasant, serious women with sturdy flat-heeled sandals and open faces; since their food arrived at the same time as his, since the restaurant was full and other people anxiously searching for a free table, since it was so nice to be talking like this (and since – presumably – a lot of other things), they suggested that he move to their table and join them. After they had separately paid their separate bills Robert invited them to have coffee with him at a quieter place he had discovered away from the port.

And one thing leads to another. In short, one of the women made her excuses and bade him goodnight and Robert found himself accompanying the other back to her hotel room. When he left some time later he thought he caught a glimpse of the first woman sitting reading on a sofa in the lobby, then, as he got into the car, suddenly realised that of course they shared the twin-bedded room. It occurred to him that they must have made some prior agreement, he tried to remember whether they had both retired to the ladies' lavatory at the same time, wondered in effect who had chosen whom. In the end it did not seem to matter. What a pity they were leaving the following day, she had said, to which Robert had agreed politely.

3

'Logically speaking,' wrote Chloe, 'it cannot very much matter what is done with a body after death. And yet, and yet, all things being equal, burial is really preferable to cremation. Earth to earth, ashes to ashes, dust to dust – but it is somehow more decent if this process is allowed to happen slowly in the ground rather than hastened in some dreadful kind of oven. Burial grounds are peaceful places: lichened gravestones, their inscriptions gradually blurred then obliterated by time, their owners in the end forgotten. A "garden of remembrance" is a terrible thing: much better not to be remembered. If I cannot be buried in this garden, then I'd like to be put right in the far corner of the village graveyard, beneath the cypresses.'

To Robert, when he began working in the garden, she said, 'By the way, please don't disturb the graves.' He looked puzzled. 'They are in the corner of the garden where the white irises grow.' Then, after a moment, 'Silly of me, of course you haven't seen them flower yet, so you don't know which ones are white. It is the east corner. They are Turkish graves, five of them. The Turks,' she added sternly, 'are a civilised people who had the civilised habit of burying the dead in their own gardens where they belonged.' She seemed curiously vehement about it.

'The Church is very adamant about people being buried in hallowed ground. If one were going to be a tiny bit cynical, one might think it was because they didn't want to miss out on burial fees' – thus spoke Anthony. 'How she ever managed to get permission to bury whoever he was in her garden heaven only knows. They do say that she went and bearded the Bishop in his den – very appropriate expression, that – and wouldn't leave until she'd got the right bit of paper. Now of course she *might* have managed it by feminine charm alone, which apparently she did once possess in great measure' ('Still does,' murmured Robert, suddenly realising it) 'but the more probable version is that she blackmailed him. Something about a compromising photograph that she acquired from a boy in her village. She has the reputation of being a bit of a witch when it comes to knowing other people's business.'

When Chloe started writing in what was to be the first of many exercise books (with ruled lines and bright-blue plasticised covers – the cheapest kind used by Greek schoolchildren), what she had written was lists. An account-book of life that accounted for nothing, recounted nothing: obsessive inventories, sometimes of furniture or objects in the house or books but mostly of the garden, of plants currently existing, of plants that might once have existed, and gradually – as some sense of the future began to reassert itself – of plants that might one day exist. 'There is a pathetic need to seek refuge in order, a madness in the desperate urge to try and impose control on chaos,' she recognised wryly as she caught herself heading a page 'Things to be done', yet could not stop herself. Later on the lists were superseded by neat plans and carefully labelled diagrams; the fourth exercise book was less schematic, and by the fifth her handwriting was larger and her thoughts more flowing. (Anyone perusing Chloe's notes would have noticed that the first couple of books in particular were written in a minute and regular hand: tiny, carefully formed letters pricked out in black ink upon the page.) 'You make the best of things,' was what she later thought (but did not write). 'You survive, you find whatever way you can.'

If you catch a lizard by its tail you find that you are left with nothing but a twitching tail in your hand, for it self-amputates instantly and the lizard scuttles off, mutilated but alive. Robert had been watching the small, slender, bronze-coloured wall lizards sunning themselves on the steps leading down from the terrace and had noticed that some seemed to have botched, crooked or stunted tails. He asked Chloe about it one day: 'Do all lizards do it? Can all of them shed a tail at will and regenerate it, or is it only some species?'

She paused a moment, half-smiled rather sadly. 'Do you know,' she said, 'I can't remember. I ought to know but I'm afraid I don't.'

'It's an extraordinary survival mechanism anyway, even if the tail doesn't regrow perfect.'

'The amazing thing is that it regrows at all. Can you imagine the agony of it, though? The instant of panic, and then the dreadful moment when part of your body just *detaches* itself . . . One wonders how long it goes on hurting for.'

Perhaps lizards feel pain differently, perhaps they are better at bearing it. There is in animals an acceptance of the way things are – of what Chloe thought of as the *is-ness* of things, whereby *I am* becomes less important than *it is*: you could say this is simply due to lack of imagination, although in terms of survival it might be called wisdom.

'There is panic at night and there is panic at noon,' she reflected. The night kind – the palpitating heart, the dizziness and dry-mouthed shivering – could more properly be called anxiety and has to do with self: *I might die* is perhaps the form this terror takes when it emerges into words. (You grow out of it though, thought Chloe, from the moment that you learn to say 'Yes'.) The shiver at noon comes from an altogether more primitive terror, far beyond the reach of words. For an instant even the cicadas fall silent. Might there be a sudden, brief, rank whiff of goat in the air? Gooseflesh, the fine hairs on your back erect: for a few seconds all senses strain to apprehend the unapprehendable. *Someone walked over my grave* are the words people use as they hasten to trivialise and dismiss the experience (and relate it once more, unthinkingly, to self) – but even this banal little phrase recalls the existence of other, less comfortable, dimensions. Chloe had often thought that midday is the time when all the gods visit the garden, though perhaps it is simply the oldest goddess.

'You mustn't be frightened of snakes,' he tells her, 'they won't hurt you if you leave them in peace. Anyway, this one is a grass snake, perfectly harmless.' They watch as the snake eases itself over the parapet and into the cistern. In the cool water it curls and coils and twists and turns, languorous, voluptuous among the lotuses. 'One of the lords of creation . . . he was hot, poor fellow,' Robin says. He smiles as some lines of Catullus come to mind; '. . . tuam fonticulam' *he murmurs a little later as they lie in the shade.*

He rests his hand on her breast for a moment: 'I always wonder what kind of snakes the Minoan bare-breasted goddesses hold in their hands . . .' 'On one of the islands, not this one, I'm afraid, there is a church set half-way down a rocky cliff face,' she tells him. 'Every year on the 15th of August – the great feast of the Virgin Mary – snakes emerge from the rocks and the girls pick them up and drape them round their arms and carry them into the church. I cannot tell you what kind they are. Our Lady of the Serpents,' she adds as he carefully does up the buttons on her blouse.

*   *   *

Some years before meeting Robert, Chloe had sat late one night writing about illustrations in children's books. She had been thinking of – and meaning to write about – trees, yet what emerged was slightly different.

'An illustration,' she wrote, 'may offer an initiation, an opening of the mind and senses to the possibility of a world or worlds outside the child's immediate experience.' She paused; this seemed rather vague, so she started again, using the first person (rare in her notebooks at this stage). 'There were no cypress trees in the land where I grew up. I was familiar with oaks and elms and beech trees, ancient trees some of them, verdant and spreading, dripping in the rain or bare and creaking in winter. The first cypress trees I ever saw were in a picture, an illustration in my book of Greek myths: there was a small group of them, five or six, standing tall and dark on a steep hillside, while below lay the most calm and fruitful of landscapes and a palace that beckoned one to enter. The picture radiated heat and stillness and bright light and cool deep shade; I know what time of day it was, three o'clock in the afternoon, and what time of year, July. I think that the illustrator knew about the silent time. His delicate, detailed, turn-of-the-century picture with its jewel-like colours, dark viridian trees and pure blue sky, was an erotic image. He told what he knew. And thus I was seduced at the age of seven or eight and remain eternally grateful to him for showing me, for leading me to the door and allowing me to enter. This picture was one of three illustrating the myth of Eros and Psyche. No other myth had more than two. I have loved cypress trees ever since.'

'I feel extremely sorry,' she said, 'for children who are never exposed to anything but cheap, vulgar cartoon images. Such an impoverishment of spirit.'

Robert had driven Chloe into town and they were now

returning, passing a cinema outside which some Disney film was being advertised. Robert was familiar with this argument, had indeed frequently turned it this way and that in his mind, had been through it all with Annie. However, Chloe's ventures even into this small provincial town were few and far between, her world for the most part an inward-looking one set aeons away from the pace and realities of modern urban existence, and it seemed to Robert almost impossible to try to explain to her why there is nothing to be done about it; he thus merely said, 'You can't turn the clock back. You can't expect children to ignore what is, after all, the reality of life around them.'

She replied, 'You could try to counteract ugliness and vulgarity though, by showing them something better.' (These were almost exactly the words Annie had used, although Annie had added, 'Sooner or later you will have to stand up and be counted, my love.')

'I do try,' he had said then and said again now.

(Anthony's school reports had tended to say 'Could do better if he tried'; Robert's were more on the lines of 'Deserves full marks for trying'.)

'Nobody has ever changed Madame Chloe's mind about anything,' pronounced Anthony, 'if she takes a dislike to you, that is very definitely that.'

Robert had given up trying to remonstrate at such sweeping statements about someone whom Anthony had never met. Thus, mildly, 'I don't find her particularly hard to get on with,' was all he said.

'Joachim had a terrible time.'

'Who's Joachim?'

'I mean the German who worked for her before you.'

'I didn't know you knew him.'

Anthony looked faintly discomfited. 'Oh, small town and

all that, I run into him from time to time.' A pause. 'Had the odd little *passage d'armes* with him actually, if you really want to know.'

Anthony had frequently taken it upon himself to advise Robert about his personal life; Robert had never presumed to return the favour and was thus prepared to let the subject drop. Anthony continued, however.

'He says she has a violent temper, a vituperative tongue and is clearly quite, quite mad. He says he doesn't envy you' (Robert made no comment at these present tenses) 'and if you find jewels in the garden watch out, let any rings in trees well alone.'

'Rings in trees?'

'Apparently there's a pearl ring jammed into the trunk of a cypress tree – though goodness only knows, he's a mercenary little animal and quite likely would've nicked it if he'd thought he could get away with it.'

Robert verified this claim the following day. It took a bit of searching but finally he spotted it: a gold ring with a single black pearl wedged at shoulder height (Chloe's head height?) into the bark of the largest cypress.

As it happened, he wished that this conversation with Anthony had taken place a week earlier. For while turning the earth beneath one of the hibiscuses – the orange one – he had found a wedding ring and without thinking too much about it had handed it to Chloe: this, after all, is a fairly normal thing to do with something one finds in someone else's garden. An instant chill. 'Yes,' she had said, 'yes. It was in fact meant to be where you found it. I shall be very much obliged to you, Robert, if you will please bury it again where it belongs.'

He apologised and did so. On the inside of the ring was engraved a date – just over fifty years ago – and a name in cursive Greek that he could not decipher, beginning with the letter M. The subject was not mentioned again, but a perceptible coolness remained in the atmosphere for the next couple of days. He did not, of course, say anything about the black pearl; he felt that if he'd known about it earlier he would have left the wedding ring in the earth.

Robert was beginning to understand that the garden was a place of remembrance, although he had not consciously formulated this thought. 'It's true that she is very possessive about the garden,' he wrote to Annie, 'but then why shouldn't she be? It's *her* garden, after all.'

Chloe, three days previously, had written: 'Gardens cannot really ever be said to *belong* to anyone. They are ours on trust, merely lent for a while; this is true even for a newly created garden that one has made oneself – and how much more so for a garden that one inherits, as I did this. I do not know into whose hands I shall give it. I cannot even know whether it will continue as a garden or whether it will be bulldozed one day when I am gone and turned into a building site. I can only act in trust. I have, however, felt a great need to leave it in perfect condition – perhaps in the superstitious belief that this will help ensure its survival, or perhaps merely from pride and vanity, the desire not to be found wanting as its steward – and this is the reason I decided to employ my former gardener' (*that blond brute* is what Chloe had been about to write, but amended the phrase) 'and now Robert.'

Sleepless, she wandered into the library, searched for a half-remembered book and did not find it; instead, while searching, she retrieved a small, battered Book of Common Prayer (her grandmother's, she suspected) that had been wedged behind something else. She carefully brushed the empty, dry, mud-and-spittle egg chamber of a wood wasp from its closed pages, half-wondering how such a construction can be built by an insect and why it likes books so much, then sat in her nightdress in front of the window and idly began to read the Order for the Burial of the Dead: *Lord, let me know mine end, and the number of my days: that I may be certified how long I have to live.* This, thought Chloe, is at first sight a strange wish. She read on: *Man that is born of woman hath but a short time to live. He cometh up, and is cut down, like a flower* . . . She mused on nature's rhythms, on cycles of growth and decay. *In the morning it is green, and groweth up: but in the evening it is cut down, dried up, and withered.* These were not unpleasant thoughts. Deciding that she rather liked the Prayer Book, she took it back upstairs with her.

It occurred to her that nature is probably very exact in its time-keeping, that if most children are born at night this is probably because they were conceived at night. She allowed herself to wonder when children conceived in the middle of the day are born. Her son – never carried to term – was conceived at six minutes past three on a hot July day amid the rustling and sighing of the green reeds.

'Chloe is a good name,' he says, 'the green grass flourishing . . .' Both laugh. 'And if you're wondering how I happen to know what it means' (he is teasing her) 'it is simply because I had a classical education.'

Under her instructions Robert was cutting back – hacking back – the thicket of giant reeds that had been steadily encroaching the land immediately outside the garden wall. 'If we don't do anything about them,' Chloe said, 'we'll wake up one morning and find that they've enclosed us within an impenetrable barrier, like Sleeping Beauty. Too much of a good thing,' she murmured, then, severely practical once more, 'I think you'd better wear gloves' – and set off back to the house to find some for him.

Robert was glad of the gloves, not having realised before how aggressive reeds can be. 'People often get rid of them by setting fire to them and burning them,' she had said, 'but I'd hate to do that because of all the creatures that live in them. Watch out for snakes, by the way.' Robert saw no snakes, but when he paused for a pee and a breathing space, hot and sweaty, glanced up and suddenly became aware of a small bright-green tree frog clinging motionless to a reed, at eye-level, inches from his face. (Robert, it should be noted, had never once urinated in the garden; however, the reed-bed was quite a long way from the house, beyond the garden wall, and he was certain of being out of binocular range.)

At lunch he told Chloe about the frog (cool and showered now, yet aching still from his battle with the reeds).

'Yes,' she said, 'they're quite delightful, aren't they? There are lots of them around, although their camouflage is so good that one rarely sees them. They count on it actually, that's why they're the easiest frogs to catch – they sit quite still, poor things, instead of trying to escape.' Chloe was clearly in a talkative mood. She continued, 'Normally the only way to catch frogs is by shining a bright light in their eyes at night and then netting them swiftly while they're momentarily disoriented. Many years ago I had what I thought was the brilliant idea of introducing frogs to the cistern. I collected tadpoles in the spring – marsh frogs, which in Latin are rather wonderfully called "laughing frogs". But they laughed too long and loud, I'm afraid, a terrible bre-ke-ke-kexing and koaxing, and my husband hated them for keeping him awake and threatened to shoot them one by one, so I begged a week's grace for them and caught them by night and took them back to the stream they had come from.'

Robert said nothing: Chloe had never before spoken of a

personal past, only, on occasion, of a dispassionate histori-cal past.

'I knew he meant it, you see. He could have hit a frog at fifty paces, he was an excellent marksman.'

A curious expression on her face which Robert could not decipher. Some severity in her tone: 'It is in fact extremely arrogant to imagine that one can interfere with nature, much better to let frogs decide for themselves where they wish to live. Very childish of me.' Then, with a smile, 'You probably collected tadpoles as well when you were a child – English children always do. Or did.'

'Yes,' said Robert, 'of course I did.' And the conversation moved on to other subjects.

Chloe's husband disliked frogs and believed that all snakes should be killed on sight.

In early summer they find the shed skin of a snake on the ground behind the great datura bush. 'In Greek,' she tells him, 'it is called a snake's "shirt".' He takes off his shirt: 'I want to undress you,' he says, 'I have been wondering all winter what you look like naked.' It is true that their love-making the previous summer was always in a semi-clothed state. Neither her husband nor her dressmaker knows why she has had her summer dresses made this year with buttons down the front; the dressmaker thinks that Chloe is probably in the vanguard of what is being worn abroad and thus repeats the design for other clients; without knowing it, Chloe has set a local fashion. Now he unbuttons her dress and she shrugs it off. 'Manus est cupida,' he says as he proceeds to remove her knickers. All winter long she has been trying to improve her Latin. All winter long she has been forbidding herself to think of tenderness.

*   *   *

There is a great luxury in putting on a clean shirt that has been immaculately ironed by someone else. It occurred to Robert – used to doing his own ironing, and Annie's too – that the smell of freshly ironed laundry is one of the pure minor pleasures in life. Chloe laughed when he told her of this thought. 'Yes,' she said, 'and the other two clean and happy domestic smells are freshly mown grass and freshly baked bread.' (There was no grass in her garden and bread was usually bought from the baker in the village.)

Robert was in fact not at all used to being waited on; well trained by a series of women – mother, wife, Annie – he automatically cleaned the bath and set the towels straight and made his own bed each morning. What Maria thought of this is unknown since she never expressed it: amusement, approval, disapproval? But once a week she set up the ironing board in the little room beside the kitchen and ironed his shirts with finely judged impassive expertise, so that he scented their fragrance as soon as he came upstairs to wash before lunch. In this household, Robert noted, shirts were not folded and placed in drawers but were hung on hangers in the cupboard.

And in this household duvets were clearly not used; one day Robert found two heavy woollen blankets, smelling faintly of lavender, folded at the foot of his bed.

Now beds are a subject you have to be careful with when illustrating books for children, since you do not wish to give anybody the wrong idea or present anything that might be open to misinterpretation. Robert, who during the last couple of weeks had been working on the illustrations for a book self-consciously designed to familiarise children with the idea of illness, recognised with amusement that he had been drawing a series of black, white and brown children tucked up in neat, chaste, *blanket-covered* beds of great repression.

At home he might have shared this thought with Annie and she might have laughed. He decided to scrap the drawings and start again with something a little less timid – perhaps the blankets could at least be untucked and rumpled. But one thought leads to another: Annie's warm, comfortable shape beneath a rumpled, warm and comfortable duvet.

Nevertheless, he was at any rate glad of these alien blankets; mornings in the garden were still hot but dusk fell earlier these days, he put on a jacket for dinner now, and the nights were getting cool.

'Poor you,' said Anthony, by whose fax machine Robert kept in touch with his agent. 'I'm so glad I've never had to agonise over the finer points of political correctness.'

What Robert was suddenly agonising about, however, was the possibility that he might have forgotten to put away his drawings before leaving. He had been making a pen-and-ink sketch of the view from his window, but also a couple of detailed erotic drawings (the woman bending forwards, the man behind her: Annie's curly hair and plump bottom). He very much hoped that neither Chloe nor Maria would find reason to go to his room that afternoon.

When he got back he ran upstairs anxiously and was relieved to find his drawings neatly put away in the battered folder in which he usually kept work-in-progress (where, as it happens, Chloe had quietly placed them an hour and a half earlier).

'Classical education or not,' she says, 'I refuse to believe they taught you that at school.' The first end-of-summer rain has fallen torrentially that morning; the sun is out now and the ground is steaming, but in the reed-bed it is still too damp to lie down. 'This,' he has just told her, 'for the ardent but impoverished client of a prostitute in ancient Athens, was the

cheapest position.' 'You made it up,' she accuses him now. But, 'No,' he says, suddenly young and serious and smiling, 'I promise you I didn't. They called it the bent-over position and it cost half a drachma. I must have read it somewhere,' he adds. Autumn is coming and he will leave: a sense of urgency, a sense of sadness.

The truth is that Chloe had several times been to Robert's room in his absence and scrutinised his work. She was perfectly aware that he was in some senses a guest in her house, that this was in any case an unforgivable invasion of his privacy, yet the impulse that made her do it was apparently a strong one. Once she had read an unfinished letter left lying on his table. She had also read more than one of Annie's letters which she found in a drawer; had he kept a diary there is no doubt that she would have found and read this too. Twice she had opened the cupboard and looked at his clothes – looked, not touched – and breathed in the faint scent of maleness that emanated from them.

People's fantasies are private things. The instinct which had made Chloe put Robert's drawings away in his folder was in some strange way a sense of protectiveness, a desire that he should not be laid open, exposed and vulnerable, to anyone but herself – illogical, of course, since it was only she who pried into his possessions. But this feeling resulted in a certain tenderness for his vulnerability and – more importantly – in the satisfaction of whatever need had made her spy on him in the first place, so that in fact she never again visited his room while he was out. Nevertheless, she continued to watch Robert at work and noted each detail of his body in a way that would certainly have made him embarrassed and uncomfortable had he been aware of it. To Chloe this observing was both comfortable and comforting.

4

As autumn advanced, the town gradually emptied of holiday-makers, breathed a sigh of relief, and put on its serious, bustling, real-life face. At the little restaurant on the port Robert now sometimes sat inside; one of the waiters warned him that, come mid-November, it would be closing until spring. Shop windows were suddenly full of winter clothes and – in spite of the fact that the schools had already opened again after the long, long summer vacation – of the kind of paraphernalia that schoolchildren seem to require afresh each year: rulers, pencil cases, satchels, many of them decorated with crude images from the latest Disney film of which Chloe had disapproved so much. The open-air summer cinema closed and its winter counterpart opened, proclaiming a new sound system and complete refurbishment. Robert went to see a film one Saturday evening and found himself in a world of frilled and ruched crimson curtains, of synthetic silk and deep plush seats, a nightmarishly womb-like overheated atmosphere that resembled what he had always imagined the decor of a turn-of-the-century brothel to be like (fantasies being not only private but often of many-layered complexity where fear and attraction coexist); in any case, everyone in the audience seemed very much younger than him, he felt he had already seen one car-chase too many, and left half-way through the film. The cool fresh air outside was a relief. The sound of his footsteps in the silent street.

*   *   *

And work in the garden proceeded. 'This year,' Chloe declared, 'we shall be serious about making leaf-mould.' On her instructions Robert began digging a large square pit outside the garden wall, in the space made by clearing the reeds. At first he tussled with roots, then dug down into black earth, then realised it was ash, then reached the layer of unburnt rubbish: old tin cans and broken glass, buried at least two feet deep. Some of the broken glass still had labels that were legible. They were in German.

'I see,' she said when he told her. 'Well, they were nothing if not thorough, even in disposing of their rubbish.' She did not seem particularly surprised.

Robert suggested that he could remove all the rubbish carefully.

'No, much better leave past history buried. I think we'll just have to make a leaf-mould pit somewhere else.'

At dinner she explained. 'They took over this house during the Occupation,' she said, 'and used it as their local headquarters. I'd forgotten that you probably didn't know. When everyone remembers something, no one bothers to speak of it,' she added. Or cares to.

He risked asking, 'Were you here then?'

'Yes, oh yes, we were here.' A silence. Then, wryly, 'It is rather amazing how old passions surface when you're not expecting them. I lost my temper with that young man who worked here before you came and heard myself, I have to admit, using the most appallingly racist epithets. Oh dear. Not that he didn't deserve them . . .'

Robert was aware that she was changing the subject and wondered if he was about to learn of Joachim's third and greatest crime.

However, 'He plays the piano in a rather dubious bar these days, I believe,' she noted reflectively – and the conversation was apparently closed.

Ten minutes later, though, as she put down her empty coffee cup, Chloe suddenly smiled and added, 'Heavens, I really don't know why I call it "dubious", because actually as far as I can gather there's not the slightest doubt whatsoever about that bar.'

It is the things that people only half-remember that are spoken of. And the gaps in memory are mended, amended, embroidered sometimes or sometimes plain darned: at any rate rewoven into a durable tissue that will do duty for fact. Such facts may be stored or used or handed on as heirlooms. When the embroidery has become particularly fine with the passage of time the fact is gradually transformed into myth. But things half-known and half-remembered form the warp and weft of its cloth.

Everyone beyond a certain age has things in his or her life that need to be reworked: irregularities or snarled and nubbled places, fraying edges, perhaps great rents and tears. The darning is carried out in silence; there are things that are never spoken of. And in this silence they may be un-remembered and slowly un-known until in time they can be expressed once more. Only the young will speak immediately of everything, confident in the hubris of their smooth, fresh, unmarked lives.

The true gossip is he who delights in the irregularities and quirks of life for their own sake, without malice.

'I wouldn't cross her if I were you,' said Anthony, 'because apparently she really is a witch. She put a terrible curse on some poor boy, newly married, young and fresh, just starting out on his life – his wife was longing for a baby, but it took months and months of visiting doctors before he was able to beget it. They went to Athens actually, probably felt a bit shy about consulting a specialist round here, but nothing ever remains secret for long. I believe she had to pay the Church a wacking great bribe to save herself from being burnt at the stake.'

Robert dismissed this as yet one more of Anthony's flights of fancy, though in fact this time it was not so very far from the truth.

Robert brought a barrow-load of logs over from the outhouse where they were stored – resinous pine to get the fire burning and solid chunks of twisted olive root that will glow and flicker slowly for hours and give off great heat. Under Chloe's instruction about the different types of firewood he lit the fire. On the table her diamond sparkled in the firelight; they were drinking the year's new wine. A wet and windy night.

The talk had ranged from drawing to children to parents. As so often in these evening conversations Robert was content to follow Chloe's lead, to listen more than he spoke. She reverted for a moment to the question of the Occupation. 'Maria has much worse memories than I have,' she said. 'When she gets angry with her son she accuses him of selling himself to Germans, actually the expression she uses is much more picturesque, very graphic indeed, but I'll spare your blushes. The point is that neither understands the other: he tells her quite reasonably that he has a living to make, that German tourists' money is as good as anyone else's, or better even, and that anyway he's forbidden by law to discriminate, while she points out, unreasonably but equally truthfully, that money isn't everything and that there are much older laws which should be respected. Of course the reason she gets angry with her son in the first place is that he has escaped from her control, but that's another matter – the fact is that a great gulf of memory and experience yawns between them.'

'What does Maria's son do?'

'He has a restaurant. I thought you knew, you eat there fairly often I gather.'

Another gulf of experience yawned. Robert, used to the anonymity of city life, felt uncomfortable at this reminder that in small towns things are different. It occurred to him that Chloe might very well know what he ate (quite apart from anything else).

And indeed it is true that Chloe did often – though not always – know what Robert ate, or at least what foods he showed a distinct preference for, such information being considered harmless. For of course in a world where everyone knows everyone else's business a certain etiquette has necessarily evolved as to how to handle this knowledge: what is spoken of and what is never mentioned. If, for example, you meet your neighbour or your colleague or your brother-in-law when visiting the Russian girl you will nod to each other but neither of you will ever refer to the encounter. If, on the other hand, you meet your sister-in-law emerging from the kind of hotel where rooms are rented by the hour you will be very unlikely to keep silent. And foreigners as well as women are generally excluded from this system of discretion. However, the fact that Robert ate so regularly at her son's restaurant seemed to Maria to betoken some loyalty, a proper sense of family and solidarity; thus, though she knew of the ribald speculations as to quite how he had managed two Dutch women at the same time, she did not pass these stories on to Chloe, merely reporting that he ate little meat and apparently had a weakness for green beans.

Chloe, who was – or had once been – a good hostess, reduced the amount of meat served at her table.

(Annie's daughter was a vegetarian; she was rarely at home these days but nonetheless Annie had got into the habit of cooking basically meatless meals. Robert – well brought up

– ate anything that was put in front of him, but he too had unconsciously become accustomed to choosing vegetables. As Annie pointed out, this meant plenty of material for composting.)

Chloe's exercise books contained extensive passages on re-cycling in the garden. Of course, by the time Robert came into her life her views on mulching and compost-making and leaf-mould could well have been considered to belong to the mainstream of ecological correctness: indeed, this is how they would have appeared to Robert if he had ever given the matter any thought. To Chloe, however, these practices had a deeper significance. An outward visible sign of an inward spiritual grace painfully striven for.

Thus: 'There is a fitness in the natural world,' she had written. 'Nothing is killed without being eaten. Nothing is excreted without being reused. Nothing dies without being recycled. There is no waste to disrupt the poise and harmony of life.' (At this point in her own life Chloe's poise was pre-cariously achieved by self-discipline, harmony a bittersweet gift only to be dreamed of.)

Or later: 'Perhaps effectively there is no death. Perhaps all the young gods who die and are reborn in spring – or the Eleusinian mysteries – are simply telling me to mulch my garden.' And: 'There was never any need to believe in reincarnation.'

At the very beginning however, in her list-making days, she had merely drawn up obsessive catalogues of things to be composted: 'Eggshells, tea-leaves, coffee grounds . . . newspapers . . . the sweepings from the floor, the ash from the fireplace . . . the combings from my hairbrush, the clippings from my fingernails' (my feelings, my hopes, the ashes of my life).

*   *   *

She finds him watching a tortoise delicately eating a dead shrew. 'Fascinating,' he says, 'I had always suspected that they might be fairly omnivorous rather than pure vegetarians, but I'd never actually seen it before.' He is clearly happy. He puts his arm round her. The tortoise, unafraid, finishes eating, moves off, pauses, shits copiously, then continues on its way. 'Chelonians aren't my special love,' he says, 'but it's wonderful to see the economy of nature in action.' 'What is your special love?' she asks, although she knows both answers. You. 'Oh, serpents every time.' The tortoise has consumed flesh and bone; all that remains of the shrew is its small empty skin and tail. Some time later, when they are ready to leave, he returns to pick it up and put it into his canvas bag. By now it has begun to shrivel in the sun. 'Dear me,' he comments, 'it does look rather like one of the foreskins of the Philistines, doesn't it?'

Annie tended to tell clients with new gardens, 'You must compost *religiously.*'

In autumn birds migrate and as they head southwards fall prey to men with guns. Driving to and from town Robert had noticed these men among the olive groves with their guns and their dogs, their green boots and their pseudo-military attire.

'I hate guns,' said Chloe passionately, 'I hate violence, I hate the waste of life taken for no reason. They don't even *eat* the birds they blow out of the sky.' Then, full of contempt, 'I know, I know, camouflage jackets and so on . . . Toys for little boys who imagine that if they shoot a swallow they are really rather virile.' She added, 'At least these days no one shoots anything on my land.'

'Did you ask them not to?' enquired Robert, in genuine innocence.

'That wouldn't have made the slightest difference' (amused).

'No, I did something much more effective, I cursed someone. I'd already asked him to leave the previous day so I'm afraid I lost my temper when I met him for the second time. I screamed some nonsense about him not being quite such a man as he thought, about his manhood withering – just empty, angry words, but oh dear, Robert, it seems the poor fellow was a little suggestible and apparently did have problems of some sort afterwards. I really felt quite guilty about it, but at least it means that since then no one's ever come shooting here again.' She added, 'Maria doesn't care one way or the other about shooting birds – though to do her justice she doesn't like waste and would probably pluck them and bake them in a pie – but she thinks it's not a bad idea to have a rather frightening reputation if you live alone. The one thing I'm thankful for is that the man wasn't from our village. All the same, just to be on the safe side, it seemed diplomatic to make a couple of donations to the local church.'

Robert, who had thought of Chloe's world as a simple one, revised his opinion. Chloe, who from the beginning had liked what she thought of as Robert's quality of innocence, ran her eyes over him, noted that he'd put on some muscle working in the garden, and thought that it suited him.

A few nights later, on one of her sleepless nocturnal wanderings round the house, Chloe went up the stairs to the second floor as quietly as possible and opened Robert's door. She stood for a little while at the threshold, watching his sleeping form; he lay facing away from her, his long, lank body curled up in a foetal position; a strange and tender thought crossed her mind, that he might perhaps be sucking his thumb. He sighed and moved slightly. Chloe closed the door gently and made her way back to her room.

Robert had indeed once been a thumb-sucker, just as he had

once been a bed-wetter and a nervous child given to bad dreams and car-sickness. Nothing was ever said about the bed-wetting or the vomiting, though the martyred expressions on adult faces as they changed the sheets or sponged the car seat left him in no doubt about the undesirability of his behaviour, which of course made him feel guilty and anxious, which of course led to a shaming repetition. Once in a desperate effort not to be sick in the car he wet himself instead – and then in misery threw up anyway. Mercifully such things are sooner or later grown out of. The thumb-sucking was cured, swiftly and brutally, by the rather old-fashioned application of a bitter substance to his thumbs at bedtime each night. To Annie he commented, 'When I was slightly older they probably would have put something fairly nasty on my cock too if they'd thought of it.' The nightmares persisted on and off throughout his life.

Robert admired Annie and trusted her. One of his unformulated thoughts had to do with the sense that she had opened a door and allowed him to enter a world of warmth and generosity. He was perfectly aware of finding the swell of her breasts warm and generous.

In one of her early notebooks Chloe had listed the epithets given to God's mother: *Galaktotrophousa, Glykophilousa, Hodegetria, Phileremos* . . . Milk-Giver, Sweetly Kissing, Pathfinder, Lover of Desert Places. *Portaïtissa, Chrysospiliotissa, Iatrissa* . . . Our Lady of the Gate, Our Lady of the Golden Cave, Our Lady of Healing. Years later she had woken just before dawn one chilly morning and had written: 'The greatest mistake made by Protestantism was to strip the Virgin Mary of her power and reduce her to a sort of housemaid in the attic, an extra in the divine drama. A faith without a goddess is doomed to gradual disparition.' She thought: I suppose they were afraid of tenderness, and stopped writing.

A later entry read: 'Protestants *think* too much. Protestants have never known quite what to do about saints. One of the reasons why Orthodoxy continues to flourish, it seems to me, is that no one has ever needed to think about it. Thus older gods and goddesses, demi-gods and heroes too, were effortlessly incorporated among the elastic ranks of the saints without much worry. If it is true that a statue of fertile Demeter was worshipped at Eleusis as a saint until well into the eighteenth century, then this simply goes to show that when you don't think about things you get your priorities right.' A sad recognition: I have always thought too much.

As they lie entwined she licks his small, hard young tits. 'Why do men have nipples?' she wonders. 'Too wasteful to make two different kinds of embryo, so you make one which can differentiate either way. It's the economy of nature,' he tells her. Robin likes this economy and has taught her of it. 'Do you like it?' she asks, 'Is it pleasurable when I kiss your tits?' 'A bit,' he answers, 'mildly, but only when I don't think about it. It's like something you can glimpse out of the corner of your eye, but when you turn your head to look it's gone.' What he likes is the tenderness of it. Sweetly kissing. The pattern which may be differentiated: in a little while he will run his tongue over the curve of her breast and take her nipple in his mouth.

Many-breasted, female, fertile Artemis of the Ephesians is not, of course, necessarily a tender goddess, thought Chloe. Our Lady of the Serpents.

And sexual intercourse, passionate or not, is not necessarily tender. Robert's encounter with the Dutch woman and a subsequent couple of encounters with an English holiday-maker named Jean were not especially tender, or for that matter very passionate either: pleasant and polite would perhaps be a better description of these couplings. The fact that neither woman gave him her address or asked for his was a relief to Robert, but at the same time a source of slight discomfort: the recognition that he had, quite courteously and pleasantly, been used. Incidentally, the reason why Robert never thought of the Dutch woman by name was that she was called Annicke, which gave rise to faint but persistent uncomfortable feelings of guilt. (Her bosom had been opulent; Jean's less so, though this had not in the least mattered.) A sadness.

When Chloe watched Robert sleeping that autumn night he was dreaming vague unspecified dreams of tenderness. She returned to bed and slept dreamlessly.

5

In December Robert dreamed that he had gone to visit a cathedral with his father. It was an English spring day of great beauty, not warm but with a wide, clear, washed blue sky across which the whitest of white clouds were drifting. The grass around the cathedral was a brilliant green. Daffodils were flowering. It felt as if this was an outing from school – for the blue and white and yellow and green were the clear, clean colours of childhood – yet at the same time Robert knew he was an adult. With his father he climbed one of the cathedral towers: hundreds of shallow steps spiralling upwards, worn in the middle by centuries of feet. From the tower there was a view out over miles of sunny, tranquil countryside. Robert knew that something was expected of him; so far the dream was peaceful enough, yet there was a faint peripheral edge of worry somewhere, like something you can only just perceive out of the corner of your eye. Then suddenly his father was leading him out of a little door on to a narrow ledge that ran across the face of the cathedral, hundreds of feet above the ground. The stonework was crumbling. His father insisted, and Robert knew he had to follow. He inched his way along, facing inwards, spreadeagled, desperately trying to lock his fingers into any crevice or cranny in the time-worn stone, trying not to look down. He got about a third of the way across, then the terror became too great, the vertigo overcame him and he froze, unable to advance or to go back. His father had already crossed and was calling him to continue, sometimes bullying, sometimes cajoling: in both cases full of contempt. Robert was afraid he might wet himself. At that moment he became aware of an unknown woman standing on the paving far below. She smiled at him and said, 'It's all right, my darling, if you fall you will be killed instantly, you will be dead before you hit the ground, there's nothing to worry about, it's all right, believe me, I know.' Her conviction was reassuring. Robert unfroze and continued inch by inch across the narrow ledge until he reached the other side.

He woke in the morning with a lingering sense of comfort, although it was not until the afternoon that he suddenly recollected the dream. He wondered briefly if the woman had been Annie, but thought not; it did not occur to him that the swift certainty of her words belonged to Chloe.

December mornings were crisp and blue and clear. Chloe decided that it was time to deal with the leaning pergola. 'The mistake was planting them all on one side,' she said. 'If half the bougainvilleas had been on one side and half on the other, then their weight would have been more evenly balanced.' She was running her hand thoughtfully over one of the gnarled trunks. 'I dare say whoever planted them saw them as young, slender striplings and never conceived that they would survive and grow so old' (stroking, caressing). 'I suppose it's always easier to think of the present than the future . . . A very bad habit when it comes to gardening.' This last pronouncement was made with Chloe's usual conviction and was followed by brisk practicalities and solicitude: 'Now, you're certainly going to need gloves, bougainvilleas have unsuspected, per- fectly *wicked* thorns,' and, 'Are you sure you're all right on a ladder, Robert?' (She remembered his reluctance at the thought of going up the palm trees.) 'Good. Do you know, if you don't mind, I really think I'd rather not watch.'

The plan was to remove the thick, matted thatch of dead wood, rats' nests and accumulated pine needles from the tree that towered above, then to prune the living wood fairly drastically, in order to lessen the weight on the pergola. At that point they would consider how best to haul or buttress it back into a more or less upright position.

It took three days of hard and dusty effort. Robert worked in the afternoons as well as the mornings; not only was it no longer too hot, but he had become caught up in the rhythm of the task, carried away by its impetus. The result was a sense of satisfaction in a job well accomplished, a blister on one finger in spite of the gloves, and an ache in muscles in his back that he'd never before been aware of.

On the third day Chloe came down the garden just before dusk to see the liberated pergola. 'Yes,' she said, 'it looks quite frighteningly bare stripped of its protective camouflage, but it had to be done. Thank you, Robert.' She stumbled slightly as they walked back to the house and he gave her his arm. That night she made him take off his shirt and lie face down on the sofa while she rubbed his back with some strong-smelling old-fashioned liniment. Thin ringless hands rhythmically kneading, pressing, massaging. When I was about your age I fell in love for the first time in my life: this she did not say. The following day she lost her temper with him.

'Help yourself to books,' Chloe had said at the beginning, 'only don't leave them out in the garden, please, don't leave them open face down, and put them back where they came from.'

Robert had taken her at her word. In fact that summer and autumn he'd read a lot, more than he'd done for a long time. (A lonely child once, given to solitary bicycle rides in the school holidays and voracious reading of books from the public library.) Chloe's library contained a wide and disjointed collection of books: old French novels with yellowing covers and rough-cut pages, two shelves of books in Greek that were inaccessible to him, gardening books, books on religion, nineteenth-century fiction . . . 'He did so often find such wonderful titles, didn't he,' Chloe commented when she saw Robert picking out *He Knew He Was Right*.

However, when he selected *Reptiles of the South-East Aegean* the reaction was different. He had taken it in order to identify a strange creature, as large as his forearm, seen sunning itself on the marble bench beyond the cistern, had found what it was, *Agama stellio*, had taken care not to scatter the faded, papery petals of bougainvillea that lay between the pages, and was conscientiously returning the book to its place after lunch when Chloe flew at him in icy, spitting fury: 'Who told you that you could touch that book? How dare you interfere? What ever made you think you had any right to pry among my possessions? I cannot stand people who *spy*.' She snatched the book from his hands and glared at him.

Robert apologised and left the room. Anger is confusing in any circumstances, and anger unmerited the worst of all (what is more, an angry woman may be deeply frightening). Robert felt shaken, retreated to his room, tried to make a drawing, failed, lay down on his bed, was restless, set off on foot to the village for a coffee. By now the day was fading and it was too chilly to sit outside so he went into the coffee house, whereupon all conversation ceased for a moment and heads turned to look at him; he sat at the table nearest to the door in an attempt not to intrude, felt alien, ordered his coffee and drank it feeling miserable. His unexpressed thought had been that some kind of friendship was beginning to exist between him and Chloe. He rather dreaded dinner.

Just before dinner, however, she knocked on his door. She had the reptile book in her hand. 'I have come to apologise,' she said, 'I was unforgivably unpleasant to you without any justification whatsoever. Do take the book, Robert, if it interests you.' (He felt he'd much rather never see it again but didn't want to refuse a peace-offering and thus took it.) 'Please say you forgive me.' He mumbled something as gracefully as possible.

Their meal was eaten in a strained atmosphere, both trying to make ordinary conversation. Chloe bade him goodnight earlier than usual. At the door she hesitated, came back, touched his hand briefly, said quite simply, 'Sorry.' Robert felt a bit better.

Being human, he couldn't help having another look at the reptile book before he went to bed. There did not seem to be anything very extraordinary about it: published in Edinburgh thirty odd years ago, brief descriptive text, rather sympathetic and accurate watercolour illustrations by – he turned to the front and checked – the author, one Robin McPherson. Interesting, thought Robert, that watercolours are much more effective than photographs for the identification of species. He noticed that the bougainvillea petals were gone. He cleaned his teeth and wondered what they meant to Chloe.

The lizard on the bench is lordly, brownish greyish beige, with a skin that looks curiously shaggy, like peeling bark. 'The prince of your garden, Chloe,' Robin murmurs. Then, 'It's not so common,' he adds, 'in fact I didn't know it existed on this island. It's called Agama stellio, *though quite why the agamid lizards should be thought of as being unmarried I've never fathomed.' 'If it was called* Agamimeno *it would mean "unfucked",' she tells him. He laughs. 'In that case,* puella defututa, *the species would soon die out. I didn't mean that rudely,' he adds but both are smiling and happy and he knows he has not offended her. It is perhaps because of the difference in age between them that she so much likes being called* 'puella'.

*   *   *

Robert did not, of course, tell Anthony about this incident. Nevertheless, it was probably in search of comfort and reassurance that he rang Anthony's doorbell the following afternoon. He waited slightly longer than usual for the door to be opened, didn't think Anthony was out since he could hear music, had an awful moment of feeling unwanted, realised that he should have telephoned first as he normally did.

Anthony appeared to be muttering as he came down the stairs; he opened the door wide chanting, 'out and in and down and up.' Then, with a grimace, '*Such* a tendency to live it up, *what* a reputation, *such* a need to live it down . . . Hello, Robert, come in, come up, I was having solitary thoughts on prepositions which you can share. How about that dire combination, down and out? But the prepositions I was really thinking about were attached to the verb *fuck*: what a difference between being fucked-up and being fucked-out, and what a disaster people are if they're both.'

Robert assumed this must refer to a specific person but didn't ask.

'Tea?' asked Anthony. 'It's "out" that's the nasty little preposition, isn't it?' he continued as he put the kettle on. 'Except that I wouldn't in the least want to hurt your feelings, I suspect that the best description for that vehicle you drive would be "a clapped-out old banger". Clapped-out, fucked-out, worn-out – what a dreadful collection of epithets.'

All this belonged to the familiar and undemanding context of old friendship. When Robert left an hour later after several cups of tea and a flight of linguistic fantasy on the subject of why or how a car could possibly – if you come to think of it – be clapped-out, Anthony hugged him and both felt comforted.

Robert was less interested in words than Anthony and certainly never had occasion to consult Chloe's Latin dictionary.

Thus he never smiled, as Chloe had done, at the polite euphemism used to translate *defututus* (with a reference to Catullus) and never discovered the plumbago flowers pressed between its pages, their pale blue now faded to a ghostly grey.

With time what is remembered of others' lives fades to the palest of rustling papery greys. A scandalous reputation can be lived down, critics and detractors and gossips faced down; to do this you need the courage of your convictions, you need to hold your head up and continue as usual.

'Do you feel guilty?' asked one of the doctors, to which Chloe had answered, 'Yes. Yes, of course I feel guilty, but that's neither here nor there, and moreover I completely fail to see quite why you think it's any business of yours' (whereupon she was promptly labelled as hostile and uncooperative). 'What are you planning to do?' asked one of his colleagues more gently. 'I shall go home and work in my garden,' she replied, 'I shall continue as usual.' (It was this second man who had suggested that she write about it.)

Gardening is a silent occupation. You listen to the birds and the insects. You allow a great silence to fall over the torn and ragged parts of life, impose by your silence something similar on others, while gradually you disremember and mend what can be mended. And with the passing of the years other people's memories are transmuted until only a faint, whispering rustle of what once happened is occasionally heard.

Robert caught the bus back from town, having left Chloe's car to the care of a mechanic who understood its workings. He managed to ask the driver to make an unscheduled stop to let him off at Chloe's gates and felt rather pleased that he was able to do so (although the fact that the bus driver was perfectly aware of who he was and where he lived no doubt helped);

as he got out it seemed to him that one woman was saying to another, 'Her husband killed him' (however, his Greek was not yet very good and he might well have misunderstood).

The buzzing of countless bees busy among the flowering ivy in the silence of a sunny winter day. Robert had found a dead cat lying just inside the gate and was burying it near the wall. He decided that there was no need to mention it to Chloe, who hated things being killed in the garden unnecessarily.

(Which was in fact why she rather disliked cats, holding them responsible for the random slaughter of hecatombs of birds and lizards. Her husband Michalis had once shot a cat: this, however, was for a different reason – he could not tolerate its amorous yowlings.)

'What happened to her husband?' Robert asked Anthony some time later.

But Anthony was not forthcoming, being preoccupied with his own affairs. 'God knows, something awful, some disaster,' was all he said. 'By the way,' he added, 'thinking of prepositions, it always puzzles me why "an almighty cock-up" is synonymous with disaster, when in fact you'd really think it ought to be rather nice.'

At the end of summer swallows and swifts depart. As the days grow shorter lizards and snakes and tortoises prepare to enter into a state of suspended animation until warmth and light will wake them once more. In autumn he always leaves; in early summer he returns. Gentleness is seasonal.

Christmas holidays tend to be spent at home, or at any rate with friends and family. Tourism is seasonal and Robert's winter pleasures were of the solitary kind.

＊　　＊　　＊

'I do not,' said Chloe, 'usually celebrate Christmas very much.'
Nevertheless, when Robert came down to dinner he found the
fire burning and candles lit and a bulky package wrapped in
plain brown paper on his chair. He opened it to find a polished
wooden box with a simple geometric inlaid pattern on its lid;
the inside of the lid was covered with fine leather and when
open it folded down at an angle to provide a writing surface.
'It's a writing box,' Chloe explained, 'a sort of travelling desk,
It belonged to my grandmother, though I imagine it's older.
I thought it could be used for drawing too – well, for small
drawings anyway – and I wanted you to have it.' Robert was
touched and tried to tell her so.

He had puzzled long and hard about what, if anything, to
give Chloe; he was unable to think of a single buyable present
which she could possibly want. In the end he had decided on
a small watercolour, made one autumn day, of the group of
cypresses against a dark, stormy, slate-blue sky, the pearl-ring
tree in the foreground. She looked at it in silence for so long
that he feared she might be displeased. Then, 'Bend down,'
she said and kissed him on both cheeks.

The following day she was rather distant with him.

6

'There are fashions in plants as in everything else. Some plants, of course, are lasting favourites which go on being grown: there is no courtyard in the island without a jasmine. Others may be all the rage for a while and then are forgotten, superceded by something newer, bigger, brighter. Yet old gardens which have gone quietly on from year to year occasionally contain remnants of these former fashions; in them one may sometimes see rare specimens of plants no longer widely found. In this garden there are three ornamental pomegranates of a kind that I have only ever seen once elsewhere, but that was many years ago in the garden of an old house on the outskirts of the town, and when the house was demolished the tree – for it was a single one – was uprooted as well. There are, of course, other pomegranates in the garden that bear fruit, but the three of which I am thinking now are barren. They were planted for their flowers, which are double and slightly flatter than the normal pomegranate blossom: tight, frilled rosettes, on two trees a lighter, milkier orange than the usual colour, while on the third they are bicoloured, coral edged with white. I do not know when these trees were planted, though I suspect it may have been in the first years of the century. I fear they may now be approaching the end of their lives.'

'Though I don't really know,' thought Chloe when she reread

this passage much later, 'why one should fear the death of trees. After all, trees must be born and die like everything else.'

Nevertheless she grieved when a large pine tree came down in a storm one winter night. 'I was so used to it, you see,' she said to Robert as they stood and watched its dismembering into firewood (petrol fumes in the air, the same two young men who had dealt so competently with the palms, though the noise of the chain-saw made it impossible to overhear their conversation – if any – this time).

The pine tree had brought down the telephone lines and Robert thus made his way to town in order to telephone Annie and wish her a Happy New Year. A badly sound-proofed booth in the cavernous and echoing offices of the Public Telecommunications Company where the meter clocks up units second by second is not the most promising environment for any very personal conversation; in any case the line was poor, Annie's daughter said she sent her love but could hardly hear him, Annie herself sounded cheerful, a bit brusque and very far away, and when he put down the receiver Robert felt a little disconsolate. As he left the building he passed the Russian girl, pale and without make-up, going up the steps (presumably also to phone far-off family). He wished her Happy New Year in careful Greek and five minutes later laughed at himself for feeling better as a result.

(Robert thought of the Russian girl – whom he met and greeted fairly often in the street where he parked the car – as 'Natasha'. Her name was actually Anna.)

Annie's daughter, whose name was Hetty, had made Robert very happy a year or so earlier when he'd overheard her referring to him in a casual telephone conversation with one of her friends as 'my step-father'. He had never told Annie about this happiness (and if she ever heard the word used she made no comment), for the fact is that he regretted not having children and the subject was a sensitive one; 'I am too old,' she said (although technically speaking this was not true) and various cross-currents of guilt arose.

Hetty had decided on this usage deliberately, feeling that 'my mother's lover' sounded a bit dramatic and 'the man my mother lives with' rather a mouthful. She could of course have chosen the word 'partner' but didn't; she was used to Robert and quite liked him. Although she asked no questions – her mother being clearly unwilling to discuss anything and in any case not in the best of moods – Hetty was nevertheless sorry for Robert's absence.

And he in his self-imposed exile was missing the sense of family and belonging that he had known in their household.

When he suggested that it might be fun to try to propagate the sterile pomegranates by cuttings Chloe laughed and said, 'You may be attempting the impossible, they look far too old to want to have offspring, even by assisted conception, but by all means try if you'd like to.'

She had examined Robert's passport, kept in the drawer of the table in his room, and was thus perfectly familiar with his exact age and date of birth. Her son, conceived so heedlessly with a sharp in-drawn breath, had died but was never born forty years before.

After their somewhat disjointed telephone conversation Robert returned home and wrote a long and serious letter to Annie. The fact that she had apparently done the same, so that their letters crossed in the post, was a source of some happiness: 'Don't stay away too long,' she said, among other things.

Robin's letters are of the discreet kind that may be read aloud. 'But you never wrote,' he says the following June.

'I could not,' she answers, 'for I never knew if you would come back.'

The second autumn she sends him a pomegranate. This is a message which he understands: 'Eat some seeds and come back to me for a little while.' He does not eat the pomegranate, places it instead on his mantelpiece where it dries out slowly in the warmth of the room, its burnished ruddy skin gradually becoming a dull tawny colour – an object of curiosity in those days in his northern climate. But he comes back anyway.

An object of curiosity becomes familiar in time, as Chloe could have told Robert, and a stranger is always an object of curiosity. 'It's partly because you're so much taller than anyone else, you *stand out*, Robbie dear,' said Anthony (this was a childhood name that only he ever remembered or used); by now, however, Robert had become at least a familiar object of curiosity among Chloe's neighbours, a recognisable and known figure in post office or coffee house with his long legs and (quite unconsciously) stooped or hunched shoulders, to whom people said 'Good morning'. In Chloe's garden he stood up straight.

(One of the things that Chloe had liked about Robert the very first evening when they had sipped wine on the terrace and considered each other was the way he sat with long, serious, trousered legs loosely crossed. One of the things that had perhaps influenced Robert in Chloe's favour was her neatness and stillness: close-cropped white hair, small, trim hands and feet.)

Robert himself was on the whole incurious about his neighbours and in any case unable to communicate with them very much. All the same, after weeks of 'Good morning' he had moved on with Maria to carefully practised if possibly ungrammatical platitudes and had been gratified to get a smile in return. When one day he cut his hand slightly in the garden she scolded and bandaged it for him.

'Yes,' said Chloe dispassionately, 'I believe she likes you. Actually, the sight of a lone male without a wife in evidence makes quite a lot of old women turn broody and maternal.'

Maria, mother of a family, was the only person who knew of the small, sad, shallow grave in the corner of the garden. On the first Easter Sunday after the burial Chloe had found a wilting bunch of chamomile, wild garlic and poppies on the ground and had understood who had counted the months and placed the flowers there. Nothing was ever said.

'Oh shit,' said Robert, who rarely used expletives. He was kneeling, taking advantage of the mild and golden sunlight to weed with a trowel between shrubs, and had suddenly dug into and broken two round, white, ping-pong-ball-sized eggs that were buried there. No one likes destroying something by mistake. With his hands, as delicately as possible, he explored further and found nine more eggs, mercifully untouched. He covered them up again and put a large stone on top to mark the spot.

Chloe's mood seemed to change during the course of the day: conversation at midday tended to be more formal, so that if a silence fell Robert felt that he was failing in one of his duties, whereas by lamplight at dinner things were more relaxed. In the middle of the day she sat upright and poised; in the evening she would sometimes put her elbows on the table and sit opposite him with her chin on her two small clasped hands. Today at lunch she was speaking in cool, precise tones of metamorphosis, of all those unfortunate maidens – or sometimes lovelorn youths – in Greek mythology who were turned into plants or birds. Robert did his best to keep up with her.

'By the way, thinking of birds,' she said, 'these are the halcyon days, these warm sunny days from the winter solstice to the beginning of January. Kingfisher days – for some reason that I can't remember these gentle days were a special gift for kingfishers to mate and lay their eggs safely, free from storms.'

'Thinking of eggs,' said Robert – and told her about finding eggs buried in the earth.

'Ah,' she explained, 'they're tortoise eggs.' And asked almost immediately, 'Did you break them?'

'Yes,' he admitted (although he hadn't intended mentioning this). 'I broke two, I'm afraid. I'm so sorry – I wasn't expecting them, you see.'

'Never mind, please don't feel bad about it, Robert. They were probably not fertile in any case, for if they were going to hatch they should have done so by the end of autumn.'

'Tortoises are like humans,' he says, 'in that they do not have restricted periods of being on heat but mate more or less all the time, any day, all day long, from early summer till autumn, whenever they feel like it one assumes.' They are lying in the olive grove, watching the violent and noisy foreplay of a pair of tortoises: crashing of shells, butting, biting. 'Unlike humans though, female tortoises have a rather amazing ability to carry viable sperm inside them for long periods of time until conditions are right for fertilisation and egg-laying.' (Robin likes teaching her these things.) 'Which is why solitary female tortoises in captivity occasionally startle everyone by laying fertile eggs and having babies all by themselves in an apparent virgin birth.'

'I don't like his violence,' she says as they watch the male mount his female whose front legs are now bitten and bleeding. 'It wasn't foreplay, he simply bullied her into submission.' Robin is gentle yet he would bite her harder

if it were not for the fact that he doesn't want to leave marks.

After dinner she reverted to their earlier conversation. 'You were wrong, you know, to say that all those metamorphosis myths were simply a primitive way of explaining the natural world.' (Poor Robert had been doing his best.) 'I think it was something else that they were trying to explain – or rather, not to explain but to describe. If you stop and think about it, the common denominator of all those stories is passionate sexual desire.'

Perhaps it was the wine, perhaps the intimacy of flickering firelight and lamps, perhaps some flash of perception told him that it is lonely people, cut off from most human contact, who mull over lightly spoken words in this way and pick up conversations later; at any rate Chloe suddenly seemed less forbidding, so that without thinking, quite spontaneously, addressing her by name for the first time, Robert declared, 'Oh God, Chloe, when it comes to sex I don't think I can keep up with you at all.'

At which she laughed quite cheerfully. A pause. Then, 'Did you know,' she said, changing the subject, 'that the sex of a tortoise embryo in its egg is determined by the temperature at which it is incubated?' And suddenly seemed sad when she realised that she could no longer remember whether high temperatures make males or females.

To Annie he wrote: 'I shall stay at least until the year is up, I think, i.e. summer. It's not that I don't miss you – I do, I miss you terribly and ache whenever I turn over in the night and don't find you. I miss the scrabbling of your toenails in bed when I try to warm your feet and I miss your hairbrush in the bathroom. I would willingly iron your knickers for you.' (This was a private reference: Robert had once done precisely this, so that Annie had teased him about being an obsessive, neurotic perfectionist, if not a fetishist, and one thing had very happily led to another. Among the other aspects of life that Robert missed was laughter in bed, which – as Chloe could have told him – seems to belong with love.) 'Often I long just to sit opposite you and watch you reading.' And: 'You're right, I'm less intimidated by Chloe these days and seem to get on with her OK. Probably it's just that I've got used to her.' And: 'I've been doing a lot of drawing recently – not work, other things – which I'd like to show you.'

He showed some of the drawings to Anthony, who offended him deeply by saying, 'Goodness, Robert, you're growing up.'

When Chloe spoke of gender differentiation in tortoise embryos, she was still thinking of Greek mythology, and in particular of harpies. A harpy is probably simply a grown-up, sexually predatory woman, she thought. She wondered about 'predatory' for a moment, since after all this is a very relative term and depends from whose point of view you see the swoop and the pounce and the grab. If prey and predator co-operate, then perhaps neither word applies.

Later that night she looked up harpy in the dictionary. 'Any of several hideous, filthy, rapacious winged monsters with the head and trunk of a woman and the tail, legs, and talons of a bird' said the lexicographer, and gave an Indo-European etymology to do with sickles, curved hooks and pruning. In the vulnerable moment just before sleeping, when defences crumble, she thought, 'But I never wanted to prune him.'

At this time her fingernails are longer but she takes care not to scratch or hurt or mark him.

A couple of days later Chloe surprised Robert by asking, 'Have you ever thought that dictionaries are always written by men, and that definitions given by women might sometimes be different?' (Any of several beautiful, pure, powerful, strong, winged creatures . . .)

'No,' he answered, 'to tell you the truth it's never occurred to me.'

He stands quite still as she slowly, deliberately undoes the buttons of his trousers; he watches her, she watches him, there is not a word spoken. The timeless sound of a myriad cicadas. She slips her small hand stealthily inside and both involuntarily close their eyes at this first contact. Later he says, 'Of course it occurred to me, but I would never have dared.'

'Thinking of growing up,' said Anthony, 'has it ever occurred to you that the ancient Greek system of lover and beloved is probably the best way of turning the crude, gauche young adolescent male into something approaching a civilised being?' They were sitting at a pavement café, watching the four boys who sprawled and laughed somewhat self-consciously at the table in front of them. 'Don't you think an older man is just what they need to give them that little bit of polish they so sorely lack?'

'An older woman might do just as well.'

'Well yes, conceivably, but do you *really* think an older woman would want to be bothered with them? Or even have much sympathy for them?'

'God knows,' said Robert (still cross with Anthony), and then admitted, 'no, probably not. Except their mothers of course.' He added, 'I suppose what they need is someone who'd show a certain tenderness to their little vanities and insecurities,' remembering himself at a similar stage of development: the awkward, ungainly chrysalis time between caterpillar and moth, the time when a tadpole grows tentative little legs.

'Now I come to think of it,' said Anthony, 'I seem to remember that your Chloe was once said to have a tendency to lick the extremely young into rather pleasurable shape.'

Quite where Anthony had picked up this distorted echo is not at all clear. One of his main sources was the woman who cleaned his house once a week, who enjoyed a coffee break and what she thought of as a chat at the kitchen table; however, she was far too young to have remembered all the old stories so it is to be doubted that this particular morsel of gossip came from her. In any case it was always the vagueness of information, the ambiguities and boundless possibilities of what might or might not be fact, that gave Anthony most pleasure: a delightfully impressionistic background of light and shade from which anything might emerge. ('He suffered a sex change into something rich and strange,' was Anthony's gleeful comment on one of his and Robert's former schoolteachers.)

Chloe's information, by contrast, was generally extremely accurate and she knew a few things about Anthony that would have surprised him.

Writing of amphibians, Chloe noted: 'The process of growing up, of metamorphosis from infant to adult, must involve great physical effort even if this is not consciously experienced. From conception and spawning to tadpole is one effort – and it is noticeable that after hatching from their eggs tiny infant tadpoles remain remarkably still for a day or so like little black commas; from tadpole to toad must be worse though, which is perhaps why a huge fat bulging adolescent tadpole turns overnight into the smallest and puniest of toads.'

A single affair cannot properly speaking be called a tendency. And Robin at the age of twenty-two was neither crude nor gauche nor adolescent, nor was he puny.

If kingfisher days fall in mid-winter, what might be the midsummer equivalent? A flash of brilliant turquoise, a flight, a darting plummet, a confusion of feathers: or a tangle of hair and lips and limbs, of laughing eyes, of innocence. Phoenix days perhaps, thought Chloe. The silent time, the time of peace, the sunlit, magic, dangerous time.

'I will tell you what it is like,' she says when he seeks to know (the age-old, perennial quest: to feel what the other feels). 'It is like the Gordian knot, inextricable, unbearable, pulled tenser and tighter and ever tauter, till at last you cut through it and all the threads untangle.' She is speaking of her body, but also of her heart, her mind, her soul.

The time of focused silence where the threads are scarlet and purple and brilliant turquoise blue, before and after which stretch years of homespun yarn. Remembered time.

A person far off lives twice – once in your mind and once in that separate parallel existence of whose minutiae you may know little or nothing, in what is called real life. Sometimes you are not sure if you can fully recall a loved face: the more you strive to see it, the further it recedes into shadow. Sometimes the movement of a stranger's shoulders, a turn of head, a footstep even, make memory ache.

Robert possessed three photographs of Annie, yet when he looked at them they never seemed quite real.

'Places cease to exist when you are not in them,' was what he said to himself, 'and then click back into reality when you enter them once more.' This thought was triggered by a moment of anguish as he remembered Annie's house – the street, the tiny front garden, the doorbell, the barley-sugar columns on the porch, the twining clematis – and felt that the memory was of a place visually *imagined*, rather than a place which actually had a concrete existence in time and space while he was thinking of it. The anguish and the fact that what he was remembering and imagining was the entrance to the house rather than its interior perhaps had to do with various nightmares about being excluded, although this was not something that occurred to him.

Robert had lived in Annie's house for just over six years. It may be that a certain insecurity is always involved when you live in a home created by someone else: a feeling that you are there on sufferance and might at any moment be asked to leave (his worst dream had been that Annie changed the lock so that his key no longer opened the door, and when he rang the bell no one answered although he could hear music and voices and knew that she was in). Robert drove Annie's car when she didn't need it herself. Annie's first move remained an extremely exciting memory, although he had never told her this. Among the reasons why Annie snapped and Robert grew apologetic may perhaps have been obscure questions of territoriality, the fact that they had never set up a new home together. 'I know it's small,' she had said, 'but I worked bloody hard for it and I like it. We'll manage – we can make space for you to work.' And so they had.

Annie presumably had more space now, with Robert away and Hetty at university.

Robin's son, also at university, was conceived and born (small and premature) twenty-two years earlier when his father had long since given up hope of siring any male offspring, his only other living child being a daughter ten years older named Lacerta (who had long since become resigned to the fact that everyone called her Lassie).

7

The gate was kept locked and had no doorbell, so he might very well have turned up, puzzled how to get in or how to attract attention, then gone away again; alternatively, being a resourceful young man, he might have set off round the perimeter of the garden in search of a spot where he could climb the wall. As it happened, however, he arrived at the gate just as Robert had driven in and was closing it behind him.

'I can't let you in,' said Robert in answer to his request to see the garden, 'I'm sorry, but the owner doesn't welcome visitors.'

'Are you the owner hiding behind an impersonal third person?'

'No, I'm simply the gardener.'

'Not even just a very quick look?'

'I'm afraid not. Sorry.'

'I see. Well, I'm sorry too that you can't let me in, but as I'll be here for the next couple of months doubtless I can try again.' And Jeremy smiled cheerfully and set off back down the road.

Once Chloe's thoughts about locks and keys had had nothing to do with exclusion but more to do with match and fit, with entering, inclusion. If she now kept her garden locked it was because the only person who possessed the key was long gone.

*   *   *

Chloe believed it was thoughts of her own impending death which led her to want to set the garden in order. Chronologically, however, it was another death that coincided with her decision to hire Joachim (just as it was a killing of a different kind that made her fire him); indeed, it is not impossible that this death led to a sudden new sense of urgency which clouded her judgment, for under normal circumstances it is very likely that Chloe would have rejected Joachim straight away, not generally having a taste for the intrinsically meretricious arrogance of one who has been too widely desired. But mourning may impede awareness.

Joachim was unaware of many things about Chloe, and where he thought he understood was mistaken. He was aware of her binoculars: this seemed familiar territory to him to which he responded, for after all there can be flirtation in the manner in which a T-shirt is removed, in which muscles are stretched or various parts of the anatomy scratched long and lovingly. The knowledge of being watched explained his other displays – the glorious, provocative pissing on the box hedge below her window, a couple of leisurely masturbations ('Give the old lady what she wants') although by pure chance Chloe did not witness either of these (and Maria, who did, was not impressed), culminating in the episode with the girl by the cistern.

'You are a defiler, a desecrator,' she spat, 'a mindless, stupid, vain little killer.'

For it was a death brought about by blows from a spade that made Chloe fire Joachim on the spot.

'It was the most poisonous kind of all,' he started to say in self-defence, actually feeling rather proud of the mess of blood and skin on the earth beneath the cypress tree yet doubly defensive since he imagined she knew what he had been about to do when the snake slithered its leisurely way across the path in front of him.

'You enjoyed doing it,' she accused, 'the only things you know are ugliness and hatefulness and brutality.'

A guilty conscience makes people shift from defensiveness to aggression. Joachim, who had been on the point of attempting to prise Chloe's pearl ring out of the cypress bark, responded to her declaration that apart from anything else she didn't particularly like him brutally fucking girls in her garden by going on the offensive: 'If you like it better I fuck a boy next time,' and then, unable to resist the temptation to hurt, 'The only thing I never fuck is you.'

So angry was Chloe that neither the absurdity nor the intended cruelty of this struck her at all. 'Thank God for that,' she responded icily, 'if, as I imagine, your sexual skills are of the same mediocrity as your heavy-handed piano-playing.' The cruelty of this took a minute to sink in. (Joachim was vain about both.)

The conversation degenerated into an exchange of insults, racist and other, followed by Joachim's departure in a taxi promptly summoned by Maria who, having disliked him from the moment she set eyes on him, was glad to see him go. Maria, however, was perfectly aware that one of his attractions in Chloe's eyes (blinding her perhaps to arrogance among other things) had been his youthful and admittedly shapely body; Chloe herself would have denied this.

Approximately two months before employing Joachim, Chloe had gone into town to transact various pieces of business and had bought an English newspaper. This was not something she did very often; perhaps the fact that she did so on that particular day and thus acquired that particular issue of the paper, dated two days earlier, was one of those fortuitous comings together of events or people or things that are commonly known as fate. She kept the newspaper until evening and started reading it in her bedroom, sitting in her nightdress in front of the open window through which the cool spring air brought fragrances from the garden. The piercing sweetness of the lemon tree in flower.

She started reading from the first page, scanning news that seemed as irrelevant as it was remote from her. A right-minded (if a touch self-righteous) leading article on perils in store no longer moved her: 'I shall be dead by then' is after all a great corrective to other worries. Reviews of films you will not see, criticisms of books you will not read make that outside world seem intricate and tiny, worthy of curiosity or study yet unreal. She turned the page. Obituaries of unreal people who have died.

'Distinguished herpetologist . . . Much loved by colleagues and students . . . Born teacher . . . A dry and sometimes bawdy sense of humour . . . Life-long love of the classics . . . Vivid contemporary translations of Martial and Catullus, his untimely death depriving us of his long-planned translation of Juvenal . . . Survived by his wife and two children . . .' And then back to the beginning: 'Robin McPherson has died at the age of sixty-five after a brief illness.' His untimely death depriving me of the knowledge that he existed.

Chloe sat extremely still in front of the window. A long time later, realising that she was cold, she went down to the kitchen and made a pot of tea. When Maria arrived in the morning she scolded at the slipperless feet and the stone-cold, untasted teapot. 'I was so used to the fact that he was alive, you see,' said Chloe, without explaining who or why.

Sometimes it is hard to recall a beloved face. The photograph in the newspaper, forty years older, does not help. Something is missing – light, movement, laughter, his soul: the photograph looks very dead.

'They died two thousand years ago,' he says, 'yet because

they wrote what they felt something lives on.' He is trying to tell her what he loves about the poets whose words he quotes to her. 'They were alive, they had stomach aches and fears and desires. Oh Chloe, they seem so familiar because I know how they felt. They say the things that I might say.' (Da mi basia mille . . .) He is not satisfied with this and tries again. 'When you and I are long dead and forgotten – our brief light extinguished – someone else may lie here and say the same words. But if anything of what we said lived on, then those other people would smile as they recognised what we felt.'

When a long-known tree falls it alters everything, leaving a cruel gap in the familiar landscape.

Wild, wet weather after the halcyon days. Anthony lay in bed with bronchitis, feeling sorry for himself. ('Please bring me some chocolate, Robert, the dark kind, I need comfort food.') Since there was little that could be done in the garden in the rain, Robert visited him every day and brought other provisions as well as chocolate. 'I prefer the kind wrapped in blue paper,' said Anthony, 'but thank you anyway' (this last added a trifle grudgingly).

There is something rather miserable about being ill in bed when you live by yourself, which is probably why Robert was not put off by this crabbedness and merely answered, 'All right, I'll get that sort next time.' But fractious moods are sometimes eased by a good gossip. The conversation had turned to firearms, Robert commenting that all the signs along the country roads admonishing 'Do not shoot indiscriminately' were peppered with bullet holes.

'Goodness yes, it's remarkably foolish of the authorities,' said Anthony, 'there's nothing like a prohibition for putting ideas into people's heads. Anyway, everyone round here loves having their finger on the trigger – they'd just as soon be without their penises as without their shotguns and rifles – great fun is had firing off round after round into the air whenever there's something to celebrate. It makes life terribly dangerous sometimes, on New Year's Eve I must admit I really felt quite *timid* as I made my way home amidst a positive orgasm of bullets.' (A slight exaggeration here, since what he really meant was a hail of blank cartridges.) 'Amazing actually that people don't kill each other by mistake more often, though of course they *do* kill each other on purpose from time to time.'

Robert asked something he'd been wondering about: 'Did Chloe's husband kill someone?'

'No,' said Anthony judiciously (sitting up in bed and looking much more cheerful), 'I don't *think* so, as far as I know it was only himself that he shot.'

Relieved at Robert's general inoffensiveness, Maria said approvingly, 'He's a gentleman' (or words to this effect), at which Chloe snapped, 'I never asked your opinion.'

Forty years earlier, mother of young children, Maria had kept silent in spite of disapproving, had not even said, 'You should be more discreet.'

'When your tender little image of yourself is injured,' Anthony went on, 'your sense of self-pride or whatever, it does make you feel rather impotent. Hasn't anybody ever made you feel a bit *reduced*, Robert? Haven't you ever felt like doing something rather drastic to restore the balance?' He didn't wait for an answer, suddenly recollecting that Robert's former wife had made reduction and belittlement into a fine art. (Anthony was not usually clumsy.) 'Personally I wouldn't know how to fire one of those things – probably do myself terrible damage if I tried – but Madame Chloe's husband was born and bred round here, so he just picked up his gun and pulled the trigger and honour was satisfied.'

'But why?' asked Robert.

'Oh, I'd think she was carrying on right under his nose, wouldn't you? Casting discretion to the winds.' (The source for this was Anthony's cleaner's mother-in-law.) 'A cold-blooded lady, your Chloe.'

There were subjects about which Chloe avoided writing. Yet much earlier, in her more schematic days, she had once suddenly made a list of the places in the garden where she knew that reptiles hibernated (and then never looked at this page again). 'I'd prefer it if you'd wait till the days are warmer,' she told Robert when he suggested dealing with the large pile of brushwood that had accumulated near the compost heap, 'tortoises hibernate there, you see, and sometimes the odd snake.' She noted his instinctive reaction. 'There's no need to be frightened of them,' she said, 'snakes won't hurt you if you don't step on them or put your hand on them inadvertently – not even the horned viper which is the most poisonous one.' And after a moment added very quietly, 'They never seek to harm you. Step back and make way in due humility if a snake crosses your path.'

'They are the lords of creation, Chloe. Step back and make way in due humility if a snake crosses your path, for it will never seek to hurt you.'

'It's very beautiful,' said Robert, 'I've been admiring it, but what is it?' (He felt more confident with Chloe by now and thus was less afraid of admitting ignorance; perhaps this had something to do with Anthony's pronouncements, although Robert had difficulty identifying the Chloe of this gossip with the small, stern, dignified figure of his employer.)

'It's a clematis,' she answered, 'one of the few that do well in this climate – not one of the hybrid kind that twine cosily over suburban trellises and porches in England but a native species. It is, as you see, very rampant.' She laughed. 'It could well be another of the Sleeping Beauty plants, because although it looks more modest and chaste than the reeds it's just as inexorable.'

The clematis sprawled in a great tangle outside the garden wall from where it had succeeded in gaining a tendril-hold in a large, woody old almond tree that grew within the wall; Robert had been enjoying the swags of its greenish-cream downward-looking flowers in the bare branches. By now these were almost over and tasselled seedheads had formed, while the almond in turn was beginning to flower. Chloe assessed the situation for a few minutes. 'No,' she pronounced, 'it's a successful symbiosis, the tree is well able to hold its own – we can spare the secateurs this time.'

The rain had stopped. Birdsong and the pale-pink blossom of the tenacious almond tree lit by brief sunlight against a stormy sky. They were making one of those periodic tours around the garden during which Chloe decided upon the work that should be carried out in the coming few days.

'What I would like you to do though is to thin the lotuses in the cistern – they're terrible thugs and I've left them to their own devices for far too long.' She added, 'It would be quite a good idea to do it before the toads start spawning.' Then, doubtfully, 'On the other hand the water *is* rather cold still – I certainly don't want you getting pneumonia or anything like that, Robert.'

'I'll give it a try,' he replied. 'I can probably manage.'

'I like tenacity,' she said as they made their way back to the house; it was not clear to him whether she was referring to plants or to humans.

*   *   *

If you caught pneumonia I would look after you. I would bring you hot drinks with honey in them, I would put my arm round your shoulders and help you sit up to drink them, I would cocoon you in soft pillows and warm blankets, I would smile at you. I would enfold you in my embrace.

Chloe was irritable and edgy at lunch. Without thinking too much about it, Robert felt that the best way to deal with these moods was to thank her politely and formally for the meal, decline coffee, and retreat to his room.

He attempted to tell Annie about the winter colours: 'Even the lightning is an extraordinary neon pink,' he wrote. 'The sky and the clouds range from navy blue to slate to ash grey – constantly changing. I'd never imagined it could rain so much. I'd never imagined it could blow so much. I'd never imagined weather could be so dramatic or sunlight – when it shines – so theatrical. Olive trees seem much darker and greener in the wet, yet when the wind blows and tosses them about they look silvery again.'

('Did you imagine, Robert, that the Mediterranean was only sun and sea and sex and azure skies?' asked Anthony sternly.)

'Sex is in short supply,' Robert might have written, but of course didn't. He ended his letter simply, 'I miss you. All my love.' Later that evening, before going to bed, he began making a rather complicated Valentine's card in which some of these feelings were expressed.

Annie wrote back, 'I liked your letter. It cheered me up, since here everything is utterly monochrome and nothing but drizzle. We've both got flu, but I dare say we'll recover – as a matter of fact I'm awfully glad Hetty's at home at the moment so that I can mother her a bit. What I've really been feeling like is giving up and hibernating.'

* * *

His letters are matter-of-fact although Chloe can read between the lines. She does not often write to him. Once, however, in a moment of weakness during the long months of suspended animation she gets out of bed quietly in order not to wake her husband, goes downstairs to find pen and paper and quotes Sappho to him: 'The moon has set, and the Pleiades. It is midnight. Time goes by and I lie alone.' She knows he will recognise the words, adds nothing further. She has yet to learn the absolute aloneness of lying in bed beside someone who hates you but no longer speaks.

I never sought to hurt him or humiliate him, she thought later, I never wanted to harm either of them.

Robin was dead and buried; Robert was helping Chloe set her garden in order. In the months following his arrival some of the taboo subjects mysteriously became approachable, albeit in a peripheral manner. Thus one winter night she had sat up in bed with a shawl round her shoulders and her feet on a hot-water bottle and started writing about hibernation.

'For warm-blooded mammals like bears or the humbler hedgehog hibernation is presumably a strategy with which to face unpromising circumstances of cold and potential hunger: a sort of energy-saving device. For reptiles there is no choice: if you have no inner means of regulating the temperature of your body you have no energy to save except what is provided from outside – you are at the mercy of the elements. You cannot help but slow down as the weather becomes cooler; all you can do is find a sheltered spot in which to lie as your metabolism winds down almost to a halt.'

You wait for the prince to come and wake you with a kiss: this she was unable to write. Nevertheless at the beginning of February, just after receiving Jeremy's letter, she reread these preliminary thoughts on hibernation and added, 'It is not right for human beings to hibernate. It is not right to be at the mercy of the elements.'

For Jeremy, resourceful and determined to get into the garden, had established that Chloe was still alive and had written to her. That it had taken him a couple of weeks to do so was merely due to the fact that he had been in bed with flu, coughing and sneezing rather uncomfortably in the cheap *pension* where he was staying; however, his youth and possibly his fair hair touched some maternal spot in his landlady, so that she brought him chamomile tea and soup and dog-eared paperbacks left behind by other tenants (detective stories mostly and thrillers, which Jeremy devoured in something of the same way that Anthony had gorged on dark chocolate).

The fact that he dated his letter 'Candlemas' predisposed Chloe in his favour. The feast of the purification of the Blessed Virgin Mary. How strange to consider that women should need purification after childbirth.

'Earth is cleansing. Americans who call it "dirt" have lost all contact with reality.' This Chloe had written shortly after she had taken off all her rings, cut short her fingernails, cropped her hair (private penances perhaps, or merely mourning), at a time when working the earth seemed the only kind of purification available to her. At the end of summer the ground is dry; she watered it slowly and thoroughly and savoured the scent of hot, thirsty earth drinking. A libation. When the autumn rains started she stood in the garden motionless, getting wetter and wetter, her thin dress clinging to her body, and this too was a kind of purification.

The oldest goddess of all drinks blood as well as water. Serious gardeners buy sacks of dried blood with which to fertilise their gardens. But anything organic may be put to good use by the soil.

'Ahh,' he groans, then says, 'Oh hell, I'm sorry.' By one of those awkward miscalculations he has just ejaculated on the ground. She is touched by his confusion and tells him, 'Never mind, you have fertilised my garden.' A minute or so later he says ruefully 'Una est nec surgit mentula, I'm afraid,' and then, seeing that she needs a translation, tells her, 'It means "whoops, I've only got one cock and it won't stand up" – or not right now anyway. It's Martial,' he adds, 'and I must say, I know just how he felt.' They lie close in each other's arms and laugh quietly.

Robert, who would never have presumed to pick flowers from the garden, brought Chloe a small bunch of mauve anemones that he had picked as he walked back from the post office.

'How lovely,' she said, 'thank you,' and put them in a glass on the dining-room table. She seemed slightly distracted; as they sat down for dinner Robert felt that there was some effort behind, 'How clever of you to guess that I like the mauve ones best.' What she did not say was that when they fall the petals of the red ones always look like drops of spilt blood. Chloe thought but did not speak of Adonis. 'Anemones,' she commented, 'mark the beginning of spring.' She lapsed into silence once more, continuing to think of birth and rebirth and rites of cleansing.

Altogether it was a rather silent dinner. 'A young man will be coming to visit me at eleven tomorrow,' she said finally. 'Could you please let him in.' Over coffee she added, 'Perhaps he will stay for lunch,' and it took a few seconds for Robert to realise whom she meant.

That night Chloe opened the Prayer Book and read the

service for the Churching of Women: *Turn again then unto thy rest, O my soul, for the Lord hath rewarded thee.*

She turned off the light and slept peacefully. These days she kept her grandmother's Prayer Book by her bed and had taken to using it as a book of divination, rather as Jeremy and his friends used the *I Ching*. The interpretations she made were of course entirely subjective and idiosyncratic.

8

Jeremy did not stay for lunch, the reason being that he wished to be invited back and felt that he ought not to exhaust his charms on his first visit; this was not so much a deliberate or conscious attempt at seduction as an instinctive sense that a full-frontal assault would not get him very far, although how far or indeed where he wanted to get was unclear, even to himself.

'Why did you come here?' Chloe asked (herself nothing if not direct).

'I don't know,' Jeremy answered (introducing himself, he had said, 'My father died almost a year ago,' to which Chloe had replied steadily, 'I know'). He added, 'My father said this garden was a special place.' (This statement was an untruth since Robin had never once spoken of the garden to anyone.)

'Why special?'

'I don't know. He never said.' (If you tell lies, it is better not to embroider them: this Jeremy had learnt at school.)

Chloe asked Robert if he would be so kind as to take Jeremy round the garden. As he showed him the Turkish graves, Robert was more than usually conscious of her binoculars.

The death of someone loved is so absolute an event that the human heart scurries in secret byways to find means of remembering, of recreating. Means of making sense perhaps of the life that led up to the death.

And it was only after Robin's death that Jeremy had set about investigating the possibilities of the various European university exchange programmes. He had not considered quite why, contenting himself with a series of rationalisations: to his sister he said, 'I need to get away' (which she understood), to his mother he offered variations on the theme of broadening one's horizons. To Chloe, however, he admitted, 'I don't know,' and she found this answer perfectly acceptable, recognising that it was the truth.

A turn of the head, a footstep, a mannerism: the borderline between pain and pleasure is ambiguous – it is hard to tell whether the pang of memory brings hurt or ease. As it happened, Jeremy took after his mother's family in eyes and nose and mouth – yet the lock of fair hair that fell forward on to his forehead, his way of pushing it back, came straight from his father. A voice, a timbre, an intonation . . .

'Your garden is a very special place indeed, Chloe,' says Robin, standing naked and suddenly awed, 'I don't think I would have been vouchsafed this sight anywhere else.' Some movement perceived from the corner of his eye has made him get up to investigate; now they both watch a pair of vipers coupling in the dust beneath the fig tree. The snakes wreathe and entwine without haste. He it is who had the classical education, yet it is she who remembers Tiresias and wonders if they do well to watch something so rarely seen that nature perhaps intended it to be private. 'I should not like it if you were unmanned,' she tells him a few minutes later and lays a delicate fingertip briefly on his scrotum whose skin moves instantly in response: a puckering, a faint riffling like the surface of water stirred by the lightest of breezes.

*   *   *

Testicles are vulnerable. Ovaries are better protected, for nature has taken care to tuck them safely away within the pelvis cage, snug beneath layers of muscle and subcutaneous fat.

A loved body is the frailest of vessels. This was something that Chloe had thought about.

On the evening of Jeremy's visit she was – amazingly – late for dinner. She ate without much appetite, spoke little, looked very old suddenly and pale, so that Robert asked solicitously, 'Are you feeling all right, Chloe?'

To which she snapped, 'Of course I'm all right, don't hover over me, I can't stand people who *fuss*.'

And Robert – equally amazingly – did not apologise. 'I'm not fussing,' he said, 'I merely asked because you look tired.'

'Please don't worry about me,' he said to Chloe in turn a couple of days later as they considered how best to deal with the overgrown lotuses in the cistern. 'If I get too cold and wet I'll stop. I won't come to any harm. In any case, colds are viruses – you don't catch them by getting chilled.'

(This was something that Annie had taught him, her severely rational attitudes towards illness and hypochondria being at variance with her warm and nurturing breasts. A couple of years previously when Robert lay ill in bed with a feverish cold his secret longing had been to hide his face against these breasts, to whimper and be comforted; Annie, however, had said, 'If you don't mind, I think I'll sleep in Hetty's room for a few days – I don't want to catch it.' Robert had felt rejected and unloved, so that when Annie caught the cold anyway it seemed obscurely to serve her right; nevertheless he turned to her at night in their own bed and put his arms around her in an expression of tender forgiveness, only to be rewarded by a sharp kick on the shin and an irritated, 'Oh, leave me alone for God's sake, can't you.')

'If you don't think it's too extravagant a waste of water,' Robert told Chloe, 'the simplest thing would be to lower the water level so that I can get at the roots – to siphon it off just leaving enough for the fish – then to refill it.'

'Very well,' she said, 'that seems reasonable.'

Thus, wearing thigh-high waders acquired at the Saturday street market, he spent the greater part of a day standing knee-deep in stagnant-smelling murky water, pulling and tugging at slimy roots. By sunset he had, according to Chloe's wishes, removed two-thirds of the lotuses; as he loaded the discarded portions into the wheelbarrow to take to the compost heap ('pond sludge is marvellously fertile') something glinted in the mud. Robert picked it up, wiped it, then put it into his pocket. It was a gold ring set with three opals. A couple of days later, when he had finished refilling the cistern, he threw it back into the water. He said nothing to Chloe.

Once they meet by the cistern at a public time of day, mid-morning, and sit for a while on its parapet, side by side, not touching. A little way further off the gardener is raking the gravel (faded khaki trousers, a none-too-clean vest and a straw hat). Robin is still young enough to seek to release tension through displacement activities; he spots a couple of flattish pebbles on the ground, gets up and attempts to play ducks and drakes with them. But they are not flat enough, they barely skitter across the surface of the water before sinking, leaving nothing but a spreading concentric ripple. 'That,' she says, 'is what you have done to me – a single stone causing infinite vortices.' It is a statement of fact quite simply, not an accusation. Neither of them is very happy: the gardener's presence is irksome and they will not be able to meet in the siesta hour since Chloe's husband has asked her to come and pick him up in town. Chloe takes off her wide-brimmed hat, places it on the parapet between them and slips her hand under it. After a couple of seconds his hand finds hers. They sit there, fingers stroking fingers, while behind them the fish glide voluptuously among the lotuses.

If you stir the sludge, a mephitic stench is released. There are always things that you do not wish to know, uncomfortable, sharp-edged, awkward pebbles that will never skip and skitter gracefully over the surface – you can only hope they will sink rapidly into the sediment and lie hidden there.

'Let sleeping ponds lie, is what *I* always say,' pronounced Anthony, upon learning what the waders were for.

Robert, with a sudden flash of memory, had recited to him the lines which long ago at school had been a common touchstone of ghoulish squeamishness:

> 'It may have been a water rat I speared,
> But ugh! it sounded like a baby's shriek.'

For several days the water in the cistern looked turbid. Gradually, however, the fine, suspended particles settled on to the sediment at the bottom and the water was once more clear.

Robert had felt that it would take a week of washing to remove the stagnant smell, but in fact one hot bath was enough. Being the sole inhabitant of the second floor of Chloe's house he had a bathroom to himself; at the very beginning, when his letters to Annie were still rather constrained and awkward, skirting round all the subjects that he found hard to put into words, he had described the bathtub to her with great approbation: 'Not only does it have feet – positively regal claws – but it is absolutely huge, Annie, and very deep.' (For Robert, to be able to fit into a bathtub without having to sit with his knees hunched up was no light matter.) He also described the throne-like lavatory with its mahogany seat, raised on a two-stepped dais just opposite the window, so that when seated one had a clear view through the trees down the garden to the lotus pond. 'The plumbing makes all kinds of groans and gurglings but works quite reliably. In fact it's all very old-fashioned and shabby but perfectly comfortable,' he wrote.

Robert of course could not know – and Chloe had never wanted to work it out – that it was here Michalis had sometimes sat during that last summer, with the fine German binoculars found left behind when at last they had been able to reoccupy their own house.

Michalis, an expert marksman, had taken careful and deliberate aim. If he had had his way, if his strong index finger had given the trigger the gentlest of loving caresses, then neither Jeremy nor Lacerta would have been born. There is a very nasty little sound as a rifle is armed. An unambiguous statement of intent.

There are always things it is better not to disturb.

'At the bottom of a pond,' wrote Chloe, 'there gradually forms a thick layer composed of fine silt blown by the wind, of decayed leaves from pond plants or nearby trees, the excrement of fish and tadpoles, the tiny mortal chitinous remains of all the innumerable small insects who have met their death in the water. I suppose that if over the long, long years a pond was never cleaned out, then in the end the water would become shallower and shallower as this layer grew until finally it dried out completely. All that would be left would be a basin of black, fertile soil, rich in nitrates.' Where, when the prince kisses the princess, life could start once again.

Later she added, 'The lotuses, flowers of great purity, stand with their heads clear of the water, their faintly blushing beauty reflected in its tranquil surface. Below the water, their strong, grappling roots draw sustenance from a thick, evil-smelling black slime of death and decay.'

'It's only a paradox if you see it from the human point of view,' she said out loud the next day as she viewed Robert's work. He made no answer, supposing that her mind was momentarily wandering. The breeze riffled the surface of the water; she kept any further thoughts to herself, shivered a little and pulled her shawl closer around her.

'Do go in, Chloe, before you get cold,' said Robert, who occasionally these days felt rather protective towards her.

It was probably because of this sense of protectiveness that during the following week or so he omitted to tell her about the two or three bloated corpses that he fished from the cistern each morning. (Luckily it was always Robert who was out in the garden first.)

Nature usually manages these things better and Robert was puzzled, which may be why he told Anthony about it: on being asked what he'd been doing that morning, he replied, 'Fishing dead toads out of the pond.' (A shudder on Anthony's part.) 'They're mating,' he explained, 'but the males are killing the females. I can't help wondering if for some unknown reason there's a shortage of females, because what seems to be happening is that too many males mount one female and their weight forces her under water so that she drowns or suffocates or something, I don't know – at any rate, every morning I sometimes have to prise as many as six males off each dead female, and they're tenacious, I can tell you.'

'Heavens, Robert, how revolting, not only gang-bangs but necrophilia too. What a very fraught life you do seem to be leading these days.'

'The thing is, logically speaking, matters can only get worse – because the more females are killed, the fewer there are available for all the randy males to . . .'

'Oh, do please let's change the subject, frogs are really rather loathsome creatures and their clammy sex life doesn't bear thinking of.'

'They're toads not frogs.' ('Same thing if not worse,' murmured Anthony.) 'And anyway, when the princess kisses the frog he turns into a prince.'

'Yes, and when the frog kisses the prince they both turn into queens and live happily ever after. That's *enough*.'

Chloe, ignorant for once of what was going on, told Robert, 'The females are the bigger ones.' (Beautiful, pure, large, strong, albeit wingless creatures.)

The embrace of frogs and toads – the amplexus as it is called – is indeed a close one. 'Let go, can't you, you silly bastard, she's dead,' muttered Robert as he struggled to disentangle the determined clasp of the amorous toads and to prise them apart from their ill-fated partners. He told Annie about it too, adding at the end of his letter, 'By the way, if you've still got Hetty's Beatrix Potter books put away somewhere, do have a look whenever you've a moment to spare and see if you can find the one with the toad in it. All that I can remember is that his name is Mr Jackson, and that he's quite surprisingly sexual.'

Robert, as it happened, did not go in for illustrations of anthropomorphic animals, cuteness not being his genre, yet had a great respect for Beatrix Potter. During a conversation with Annie shortly after they met he had held forth on the essential froggishness of Jeremy Fisher. 'If you'd never seen a frog,' he had claimed, 'but only these pictures, you'd still have a sort of understanding of what a frog is like – of the enormously powerful thigh muscles and the great wet leaps – in spite of his galoshes and jacket and so on. Whatever else she is, Beatrix Potter is definitely not cute.'

Perhaps Annie remembered this conversation and the circumstances in which it took place (eating hot buttered toast and jam in bed at half-past two in the morning having somehow forgotten about dinner, the first night that he had spent in her house, when Hetty had gone to stay with a friend for the weekend); at any rate she found the time to search among the boxes in the cupboard under the stairs and sent *The Tale of Mrs Tittlemouse* to Robert by express post. (This touched him.) 'You're quite right,' she wrote, 'he is definitely a very sexual toad, an intrusive male presence, saying rude phallic things like "Tiddly-widdly-widdly" and scaring her into narrowing her front door till it's too small for him to enter. My God, the things one reads quite blithely to children . . . Timid little mouse as vagina or vice versa is *not* exactly the idea I would have wanted to instil into Hetty – though luckily it doesn't seem to have done her much harm as far as I can see.' (Annie had a tendency to cross all her 't's and dot all her 'i's.)

Robert, who had vaguely remembered the large, wet, phallic, impolite toad but had not considered the tight little front door, smiled rather ruefully as he thought of these things a couple of days later and recognised yet further pitfalls in his profession. Chloe's raised eyebrows questioned the smile, whereupon he confided some, though not all, of the thought.

'On the contrary,' she said, 'it shouldn't be a pitfall but an opportunity to tell children things.' And added, 'I learnt quite a lot about sex from the illustrations in my book of Greek myths.'

Jeremy, who was a classicist and who was finally having lunch with them, laughed. 'Then your book of myths must have been rather different from mine,' he said, 'but at any rate Robert's just cast quite a new light on the pseudo-Homeric epic of the battle of the frogs and the mice.'

There was something about Annie's letter that was immensely reassuring to Robert. Perhaps it was simply that she wrote conversationally, as she might have spoken to him had they been sitting across the kitchen table from one another, whereas their telephone calls tended to be somehow stilted and awkward and deeply dissatisfying; at any rate he read warmth and intimacy between the lines and was made happy by it. For although he told himself that dreams do not have literal meaning, that they are nothing more than an expression of one's own anxieties and insecurities, a horrible and distressing nightmare – in which Annie told him quite casually that she'd found someone else and couldn't understand why he was upset – had been lurking on the fringes of his consciousness and refusing to go away.

Psyche sought the impossible – to look at Eros – and thus lost him. Perhaps the loss was implicit from the beginning. 'Psyche was probably older than Eros,' thought Chloe.

It might take a lifetime, she thought, to reach the point where you no longer need to see, where you are content with what can only be glimpsed from the corner of your eye without seeking to understand or explain.

Perhaps the words 'I love you' are simply spoken from a full heart that seeks to find a verbal outlet for its tumult: perhaps, though, they are more often said in response to some unspoken demand from the other (for affirmation, for reassurance) – perhaps by the time these words have been formed by tongue and larynx and vibrate in the air they are no longer quite true. Perhaps the essential truth of these feelings is so evanescent that it can only remain intact when you do not seek to think them or say them. Maybe this is why lovers quote poetry to one another. I never told him that I loved him, thought Chloe. But of course he knew.

She kisses his throat in a moment of great tenderness. His larynx – his Adam's apple – is another of those vulnerable male parts of his body. 'Women's bodies are better protected,' she says, 'nothing sticks out.' He is amused that she appears to have forgotten her breasts.

Thoughts about vulnerability resurfaced in Chloe's mind after the advent of Robert into her life. In truth the autumn night when she watched him dreaming was not the only time she had stood quietly at his bedroom door, the first of these nocturnal visits having been made a couple of weeks after his arrival. In summer the nights are hot; Robert had thrown off the sheet and lay naked on his back, arms outstretched, legs slightly apart, the sweat that glistened beneath the fuzz of hair on his chest perceptible in the moonlight. Through the open window came the quiet contralto trilling of the crickets. Somewhere far off the barking of a dog. Chloe held her breath, stood and watched him for a few minutes, then went downstairs, unlocked the door, went out on to the terrace and sat there for an hour or more before going back to bed. A naked man sleeping is doubly exposed.

After death there is no privacy; anything you leave behind you is exposed to the curious eyes of the living. This includes your own body, competently plugged up and laid out for burial by strangers whose gloved hands are ignorant of the history and memories of the flesh they manhandle with such cheerful absent-mindedness.

When thou with rebukes dost chasten man for sin, thou makest his beauty to consume away, like as it were a moth fretting a garment, read Chloe. Shortly after Robin's death Maria had found her standing naked in front of the mirror, had not understood but had not scolded, had simply proffered a dressing-gown.

'I suppose,' said Jeremy, 'that the death of a parent probably always makes you grow up, will you nill you. I miss him,' he added. What Jeremy did not say – because he had not quite formulated the thought – is that the death of a parent alters the balance of the relationship (for relationships live on even after death): from being a powerful presence who needed no explanation, Robin had suddenly become for his son *a real human being*, an unknown quantity full of mystery. Thus, without understanding why, Jeremy was seeking to know him, to fill the lacunae.

We brought nothing into this world, and it is certain we can carry nothing out. Except our secrets perhaps.

'Ovid has quite a long passage about not being able to get it up,' says Robin. 'It's one of his Amores – *or in this case I suppose you could call it one of his* Non-Amores. *Actually, somehow I've never really got on so well with Ovid, he doesn't ever ring quite true in the way Martial or Catullus do – it's all too contrived. Mind you,' he adds, 'of course his description of this particular experience rings perfectly true, specially when he says that being ashamed about it makes things worse.' Robin is not ashamed, has simply said, 'Sorry, it's because I'm nervous.' Nec surgit. Chloe's husband has gone to Athens for a couple of days and Chloe is now lying in Robin's bed. The idea of cuckolding his host in his own house*

makes Robin uncomfortable, whereas in the garden it doesn't seem to bother him at all; perhaps this is because the garden is so much Chloe's territory, a world of its own. 'It's all right,' she says, 'I like being here with you, talking.' They lie side by side on the narrow bed, his arm around her shoulders. She turns her face to his armpit, snuffles him. Armpits, she thinks, are secret, tender, defenceless places. 'I love the smell of your sweat,' she tells him, 'it is so utterly male.' He laughs and she lays her head on his shoulder. After a while he sleeps. She lies awake, making as much space for him as possible, scenting him, listening to his quiet, regular breathing. At dawn when grey light begins to suffuse the sky and the first cocks are crowing she leaves him; it is cooler suddenly and she draws the sheet up to cover his naked sleeping body.

9

'She is a vampire,' said Anthony, 'she sinks her sharp little pointed white teeth into whatever vulnerable young male throats come her way and drinks their blood.'

Robert said nothing.

'I haven't noticed any puncture marks on *you* yet, but maybe it's just that you're a tiny bit old for her tastes. I really do hope you're being sensible though and keeping your door securely locked at night.'

'For Christ's sake, Anthony' (slightly annoyed but refraining from saying that there was no key to his bedroom door).

'And when she has sucked out their life-blood she takes the poor boys between her determined if these days somewhat withered thighs and a terrible little sound is heard – *krits, krats* – as she snaps their backbones.'

'Come on' (impatiently) 'Chloe's simply a perfectly harmless old woman.'

'That's what people always think until it's too late' (darkly).

'In that case why did you suggest I work for her?'

'Oh, I thought it might be rather good for you – you know, make you or break you or something.'

This answer was thought up on the spur of the moment yet contained a certain element of truth; Robert found it patronising and (rather surprisingly) said so, whereupon Anthony was contrite.

'Sorry, Robbie, I shouldn't tease, you're quite right, *do* forgive me.'

Robert got his own back half an hour later by saying as he left, 'You know, I do worry about you sometimes, Anthony, you seem to have such threatening fantasies.'

The oldest goddess in the world, the drinker of blood, is at the same time nurturing and frightening.

A man may choose a partner many years younger than himself and nothing much is thought of it; indeed, he may even receive admiring comments on his virility. For the woman whose partner is younger than herself there are disapproving words, of which 'cradle snatcher' is the mildest, while her youthful lover is rather dismissively said to be seeking a mother figure.

These were things that Jeremy turned in his mind as he wondered how old Chloe was, counted the years, tried to calculate. 'I suppose it was rather naïve of me to imagine that she would tell me anything,' he said to himself.

Chloe, with the freedom that old age is allowed towards youth, had asked him directly, 'How old are you?' and on being told had made no comment, merely suggesting that Robert take him round the garden.

And she sat at her bedroom window and watched them. The white irises are quiet graveyard flowers. ('They are always in bloom earlier than the coloured ones,' she told Robert, 'they protect the souls of the sleeping dead from evil spirits.')

In the hot summer, of course, the irises are not in flower so that only their leaves are to be seen: dusty, grey-green spiky leaves rising from the knotted, half-unburied rhizomes. Chloe has been thinning them and sits back on her heels against one of the Turkish gravestones when Robin comes to find her. She wipes the sweat from her brow with an earthy hand and leaves a smudge. 'The grave,' she declares solemnly, 'is a fine and private place but none, I think, do there embrace.' 'Catullus said more or less the same, that the time for kissing is now because when once our brief light sets we shall have endless night for sleeping in.' He kisses the smudge mark and quotes reflectively,

'Nobis cum semel occidit brevis lux
nox est perpetua una dormienda.'

But what has never lived cannot be said to sleep. His tiny, bloody remains fertilised the ground for a short space and then were gone to nothingness. A not-quite-life that seeped away in pain and desolation on to the hot, dry, thirsty earth. Chloe might have remained crouching in the garden; Maria it was who insisted on putting her to bed and calling the doctor.

'Shall I thin the irises a bit?' Robert suggested one day. 'They look rather overcrowded.'

'Why this mania for not letting well alone?' (sharply). 'The last thing I want in my garden is mean-spirited suburban neatness.'

Whereupon Robert felt hurt, apologised, but added, 'I simply thought that if they were thinned they'd flower a bit more.'

'I do not care how much or how little they flower.' (To this sort of statement there can be no response.)

He would almost have been old enough to be your father, was the thought that surfaced when Jeremy told her his age.

What she told Jeremy some days later, when the conversation turned to Sophocles, was, 'Don't imagine that Oedipus and Jocasta did not both know very well what they were doing.'

And Jeremy, sitting in the bus on his slow way back to town, pondered these things and reflected, 'She must have been old enough to have been his mother.'

Chloe's body gave her one chance to conceive and then apparently decided not to bother any more. She thus had the last period of her life at the end of June, a couple of weeks before the in-drawn breath, the sigh among the soughing of the green reeds. This did not surprise her much; premature menopause seemed a logical response to the way things were that autumn.

'I never had a particularly curvaceous body,' she said, dispassionately assessing herself before the mirror, 'I wasn't ever what you'd call the maternal type.'

'You ought to eat more,' was all Maria said, not for the first time. In her eyes the main advantage of Joachim's arrival not long after this conversation took place was the fact that it meant the regular serving of two meals a day.

The ageing of the post-menopausal body involves an inner shrinkage as if some essential substance is slowly eroding away: a loss of height, an increased fragility of bones, a slackening of the flesh on upper arms and thighs, a relaxation of the muscles in the belly. Wrinkles and loss of elasticity, yet the body remains familiar nonetheless and reassuring.

Children not only suck their thumbs but also hold on to strange objects for comfort: an old article of clothing, for example, or a piece of rag. Chloe at night tended to hold on to her own left breast, right hand spread, index finger towards armpit, little finger above nipple. This was an easy, automatic habit to whose origins she had never given any thought.

Chloe's breasts, though still soft and warm, were smaller and flatter these days. Her other comfort as she settled to sleep was the placing of one small motionless hand between her legs, like a quiet little animal – a timid mouse perhaps – to be warmed and protected and held safe. A simple, primitive comfort this, closely akin to the infantile sucking of thumbs.

(Dogs protect their soft, warm bellies by curling up as tightly as possible, nose into tail. Less supple than a dog, Robert in anxious defensive moments sometimes went to sleep with arms crossed over chest, hands tucked into armpits; Chloe, however, had not happened to see him in this position.)

Robert, albeit usually unconsciously, was alert to the shapes that people's bodies make, and thus to the way they sit or stand or hold themselves.

'In her old age,' he declared, 'she never sat down in public because she couldn't bear anyone to notice the bulge of her slack stomach under her slinky dress.'

He was referring to Marlene Dietrich, one of Anthony's objects of veneration. They were watching an old film of hers on television one Saturday evening; this statement, which Robert had just made up, was probably another small way of getting his own back. (As it happened, Robert secretly shared some of Anthony's admiration for Dietrich in her dominatrix role. What he was unable to sympathise with was Anthony's adoration of Judy Garland, the much beloved little red shoes reminding him unpleasantly of another pair, of Andersen's terrifying little red shoes that would not stop dancing even when the feet that occupied them had been amputated.)

'Well, at least she would never ever have sat with her legs planted firmly apart,' countered Anthony in defence of his icon.

Robert thought about this the following day as he noted how Chloe sat – ankles neatly crossed, knees kept lightly together. He understood very well what Anthony had meant; it occurred to him that women who after a certain age sit with their legs apart have perhaps ceased to regard themselves as sexual beings: it is tired women in buses with shopping bags, having perhaps raised many children, who sit like this – women whose sole title is now 'Mother' or 'Grandmother'. He had the desultory thought that if Chloe ever sat with her knees apart it would be quite deliberate, then chided himself and censored the thought.

'Thank God at least that I've still got all my teeth,' was what Chloe was thinking as she helped herself to sunflower seeds from one of the bowls that Maria (who considered them nutritious) left in strategic places. She was in mythological mood again and had been speaking of the Minotaur. By Chloe's reckoning Theseus probably dumped Ariadne on Naxos because she was too girlish, preferring the more womanly charms of Phaedra.

Robert, as it happened, could sympathise with this version of Theseus: it was the little imperfections of Annie's body that charmed him – the slightly puckered pale appendectomy scar, the brown birthmark just above her left buttock, the mole on her right breast, indeed the slight asymmetry of her two breasts (one fractionally larger than the other, nipples just perceptibly unaligned) – but more particularly the silvery stretch marks on her belly, the plumpness of her enfolding upper arms. The warmth of a well-used ripe body in which to burrow and find ease and peace. Fertile Annie menstruating was a special delight (although this was something so private and incapable of being communicated that Robert always kept it to himself).

'It will be rather bloody and messy, I'm afraid,' she says, at which he laughs, slips his hand between her warm thighs. 'Never mind,' he says, 'doesn't matter.' Later he takes the

old enamel mug he uses for watercolours and brings water
from the cistern for them to wash themselves.

'Poor Phaedra though,' Chloe concluded, 'she ended up unlucky, for Hippolytus proved to be something of a wet rag.'

Vénus tout entière à sa proie attachée. The prey and the predator.

Of course, she mused, I suppose one should really feel sorry for that poor scared young man, clutching his chaste little balls so defensively – he probably simply didn't dare, was terrified of being engulfed and overwhelmed and annihilated within the grip of her powerful thighs.

Robin lies back lazily. 'I would never have dared,' he says, 'but I'm unutterably glad that you did.'

Sunflowers were almost the only annual plants that Chloe grew. 'I like them for their height and dignity and innocence as well,' she explained, meaning as well as for their seeds.

'The gardener's mind is always on the future, not the present,' she had written. 'The shortest span of time envisaged is the year that it takes annual plants to set seed, to germinate, to grow and flower and die. Mostly, however, one is think-ing in terms of years and decades – or even centuries if one is planting large trees. I have not had occasion to do this, having inherited cypress and pine, almond, fig and lemon, pomegranate and loquat, the flowering jacaranda and bauhinia, as well as the carobs and olives and citrus trees on the land outside the garden walls. This sense of future, of promise, of continuity must be what spurs people to make gardens, over and above the desire for the immediate pleasure they offer.'

And later: 'There is no moment at which one can consider a garden finished. Nothing remains constant; year after year things change. Shrubs take time to reach maturity, to develop their character. The knotted and calloused wood of the old hibiscuses is of greater beauty than the green and pliant stems of their younger relatives.'

The fallen pine had left a gap, an unusual emptiness of sky and light. When Chloe fretted about this Robert tried pointing out that it offered new opportunities for planting; 'After all,' he told her, 'gardens change all the time.' (As Annie had explained, 'You always have to plan at least twenty years ahead.')

'I know that perfectly well,' she answered abruptly, 'there really isn't any need to state the obvious.' Then, a moment later, 'Sorry, Robert, you're right of course, forgive me for snapping – it's just that I did so hope the trees would last my time.'

It occurred to Robert to wonder how old Chloe actually was. For a moment the half-formulated idea that she seemed suddenly smaller passed across his mind fleetingly – a momentary impression of frailness interpreted in terms of size perhaps, instantly dismissed: nevertheless a few days later Robert asked Anthony out of the blue, 'I haven't grown all of a sudden, have I?'

To which the response was a leisurely critical assessment, followed by, 'Mmm, no, at least not as far as the naked eye can see, a *slight* little increase in girth possibly – which as a matter of fact doesn't do you any harm at all. I can't answer of course for your inner growth, Robert, the last time I dared to speak up you jumped down my throat quite ferociously.'

Robert had been brought up in a tradition of well-illustrated children's books; his childhood nightmares – no longer consciously remembered – frequently had to do with that menacing, other, Rackhamesque world where malignant goblins are to be found emerging from the knotted and twisted roots of trees, where if you turn round suddenly you may catch a glimpse of strangenesses, where anything can become anything. From time to time his adult dreams preserved some remnant of this: a terror of looking to see what might be behind him. It was probably not purely coincidental that the only poem Robert remembered from his school days and indeed had quoted to Anthony was 'Childe Roland'. And the intricate drawings he had been making recently, which somehow felt curiously satisfying, drew on this frightening sense of dream-like transformation. Robert was not aware of this; it did, however, occur to him that some of Chloe's conversation had probably influenced him.

The subject of all these drawings was metamorphosis: the stages by which woman becomes tree or tree woman. Immobilisation and movement, the swell of a breast, the twist of a torso, the suddenly rooted solidity of legs and curving hips – from flesh and blood and long, flowing hair to bark and sap and the green growth of leaves.

Robert had long thought that in certain lights Annie's darkish fair hair had a tinge of green to it. And his crayons gave him elusive dream colours: swirling greens and blues and greys.

'Dryads, properly speaking, are only found in oak trees,' Chloe told him in answer to his question. The following day she said to Jeremy, 'No, certainly not an olive, what I'd like is a holm oak.' (She had asked him to plant a tree for her in the space where the pine had stood. Robert, momentarily irritated with both of them, did not identify this feeling as a minute pang of jealousy.)

*　　*　　*

The trunks of ancient olive trees (the kind which, as Chloe lamented, bureaucrats in Brussels seem determined to do away with) grow massive and solid yet twisted into the strangest of shapes. All the same, these trees are benign: even in winter storms there is nothing threatening about them. Perhaps, thought Robert, this is because human beings have loved and cultivated them so painstakingly for so many millennia, each generation planting slender young trees for their descendants to nurture in centuries to come. An act of trust.

I shall never see this pliant sapling grow to maturity.

After the night that she spent in his room they speak more of some of the awkward subjects. 'It cannot be helped,' she says, 'this is the way things are, don't fret about it.' They are once more in their nest in the reed-bed, he lying on his back, she propped up on one elbow watching him. She strokes the smooth muscular line of his flank from waist to hip, then inwards over his belly, rests her hand lightly on his penis for a moment. He is looking away from her, says, 'I cannot help being jealous.' He turns to face her, smiles ruefully. 'When I see you with him I tremble and my blood runs cold – something like that. Catullus describes the feeling.' 'I thought it was Sappho,' she comments. 'Both. Catullus translated Sappho. Ille mi par esse deo videtur – it works well in Latin.' His apparent nonchalance is a little forced. 'Don't fret,' she says again. The curved planes of her brown shoulder, of her cheek, of her breast: the strands of her dark hair falling forward as she leans towards him. He pulls her clumsily against him. She listens to his heartbeat and is moved by his youth.

The death of a parent may indeed nudge one a little further on the path to maturity. After Robin's death it was Jeremy who undertook to sort through his father's papers and thus it was Jeremy who found and read six yellowing, hand-written foolscap pages about Chloe, about her garden, about shame and loss and guilt. He read them rapidly, guilty himself as if expecting at any moment to be accused of prying. Then again, more slowly. He searched for something else, letters perhaps, but found nothing. (A sheet of paper with a few lines of Greek was glanced at cursorily, identified as Sappho's midnight fragment, and set aside to join the pile of translation drafts.) The pages were not dated but Jeremy, applying the archaeological approach, decided that from the stratum in which he'd found them they appeared to have been written around the time of Lassie's birth. He removed them, took them to his own room, said nothing to either his mother or his sister.

Speaking of Maria Chloe said, 'Children always seem to find the idea that their middle-aged parents have sex shocking in the extreme. Her older children never quite forgave her for suddenly getting pregnant when she was over forty – they apparently felt that she was making a fool of them or something. Perhaps that's why she's so attached to her youngest son. Which of course makes the older two terribly jealous.' As an afterthought: 'The fact that his restaurant is doing well doesn't help.'

'Does Maria have a husband?' asked Robert, on whom it had only dawned recently that the black clothes he had taken as a sign of bereavement were in fact standard garb for married women of her age, nothing more than a token of wifely modesty.

'She's a widow. Like me. Her husband died a couple of years ago.'

'Have you been a widow for a long time, Chloe?' (This was perhaps indiscreet but Robert was curious.)

A protracted pause so that he wished he hadn't asked. Then,

'I have been a widow for twenty-four years, two months and three days,' she declared in precise tones, reminding him of the way he used to reckon his age between birthdays when he was young enough for months and weeks and days to matter. 'One may as well be accurate,' she added.

One may as well recognise that it is even possible to be a widow during one's husband's lifetime. There is pain and fear and trouble and grief. And of course emptiness.

She folded her table napkin with such concentrated care that Robert felt his direct question had offended her; 'I am tired,' she said, 'I shall, I think, retire,' and Robert got to his feet. The offence, however, was presumably not too great, for as she bade him goodnight she rested her hand on his arm for a moment.

It did not occur to Chloe that the nights on which sleep came to her more easily tended to be those on which she had given Robert's hand or arm one of these small, brief, caressing touches.

It did occur to Robert that Anthony's account had probably been wildly inaccurate – for even twenty-four years ago Chloe must surely have been beyond the age for what Anthony called carrying on.

Some years after everything ended, Robin sat in a train watching the Indian woman opposite him and was filled with anguish at the way a strand of straight black hair had strayed from its hairpins and fell forward over the curve of her cheek as she sat reading. He traced the swell of her breast beneath the sari, shifted uncomfortably, closed his eyes; the following night he wrote the pages that Jeremy was to find so much later. Whether Robin kept these pages on purpose or whether he had simply forgotten what he had written is not clear.

As he lay dying though, drifting between various levels of

consciousness, he opened his eyes in a moment of lucidity and said, 'I suppose if you love someone it is never forgotten.' A questioning tone, as if trying to fit the pieces of the puzzle together. Lacerta who was sitting with him was tired and stressed but did her best to make reassuring noises. She assumed that this referred to her mother; in any case, by being ill and weak Robin had lost the authority of those who are still engaged in the business of daily living, and thus his daughter, though kind and comforting, in some strange way paid little heed to the content of his speech.

There is anguish so sharp that it feels like physical pain. It may seem almost too great to be contained within one small body. At the beginning, as she lay in bed at night (first alone then beside her silent husband once more), Chloe pressed a tightly clenched fist hard between her breasts in an effort to subdue this pain and prevent it from causing her body to burst at the seams and disintegrate into a bloody spillage of quivering, pulsing, raw, wet organs. 'No more mess,' she said to herself and pressed until the more localised hurt brought some kind of relief. Over the years her fist relaxed and unclenched, and her hand moved sideways until it came to rest on her left breast, above her heart.

Comfort us again now after the time that thou hast plagued us: and for the years wherein we have suffered adversity, read Chloe one night in early March.

10

Dionysos may well be the god of gardens, as Chloe had once written; if so, then it is in spring in his native land that he manifests himself in a great passionate surge of life and growth. Quickening sap rises; trees whose twigs have for weeks looked warmer and pinker when seen against the light now unfurl their pale-green leaves. There is a tenderness in this colour which Robert, accustomed to thinking iconographically, couldn't help associating with childhood images of springtime gentleness: rabbits frolicking on close-cropped turf, primroses and violets (blushing unseen perhaps), suffer the little children to come unto me, young lambs bleating. There were no primroses in Chloe's garden. Their colour, however, was everywhere: sulphur-coloured tidemarks left round the edges of receding puddles, everything covered in a dusting of pale yellow. This puzzled Robert slightly until he realised that it was the pollen from the pine trees, millions and millions of grains of it, produced prodigally with a fine disregard for wastage, with a single-minded abiding desire to reproduce. Dionysos has never been a god of much restraint, nor tender either, and the growth of everything in Chloe's garden was eager and shameless and prolific.

Robert found himself suddenly busy with all the weeding required.

Chloe herself, over one of their Lenten, meatless lunches, asked, 'Do you eat lamb, Robert?' And added, 'The lambs will be fattening up nicely for Easter by now.' Then, 'This, of course, is the main concern of the good shepherd – protecting them and fattening them up in order to lead them to the slaughterhouse – there's nothing the least bit sentimental about the pastoral life.'

Robert, who had just been recalling one of Annie's dogmatic pronouncements ('Women are far tougher and much more realistic at heart') and reproving himself for a touch of sentimentality in his images of spring, wondered whether Chloe was telepathic.

But there is another, humbler, old, old god who lives in gardens and his name is Priapus. You may come upon him unawares as you turn a corner, startled as he flashes at you. He lies in wait half-concealed among the patches of light and shade, cheerful and lewd and mocking. Sometimes an echo of his laughter follows you long afterwards.

Robert parked Chloe's car in the alley one Saturday afternoon and met the Russian girl. She smiled and said hello as usual. Robert, having made a rapid review of how much money he had on him, said in Greek in a sudden moment of inspired fluency, 'If you were still willing, I would like it.' He used the polite second person plural. She nodded, her smile wider (if it was a tiny bit mocking now it was at any rate not unfriendly), and said something which clearly meant, 'Come on,' or 'Follow me.' He followed her down the alley. As they reached her door he glanced across the road and his eyes met those of Maria turning the corner, respectable and black-clad and laden with shopping bags. Everything was instantly hopelessly impossible; Robert mumbled something like, 'Sorry, I'm sorry, another time,' and made his escape. Feeling quite unable to offer Maria a lift anywhere, he set off on foot in the opposite direction, walked slowly round the block seething with rage and shame, then when the coast was clear made his way back to the car and drove away, thinking that he'd never be able to park there again. Infinite misery.

Maria, as it happened, was not particularly shocked, was indeed rather amused than anything else and did not under the circumstances bear him a grudge for the missed lift. She said not a word about this encounter to Chloe and served at table the following Monday with an impassive face. Without thinking quite why, she consulted with one of the waiters at her son's restaurant and made great efforts to produce what were apparently Robert's favourite dishes. Green beans – just coming into season – were much in evidence at Chloe's table over the next few weeks.

'Prostitutes in ancient Athens had the words "Follow me" cut on the soles of their sandals,' Chloe tells Robin, 'so that they left their message printed in the dust of the streets.' 'Now that,' he says, 'is something they never taught me at school.' Laughing, casual conversations, easily forgotten. Yet for the rest of his life Robin experiences a pang every time he lands at an airport and sees the car with flashing lights proclaiming 'Follow me' that guides each aeroplane to its parking place. He is never able to explain this momentary stab and puts it down to the stress of travelling; 'Or maybe,' he says to himself, 'arrival – the end of a journey – always involves sadness.'

Robert got back to Chloe's house just about dinner time on that spring Saturday; he told her that he had already eaten (which was a lie). He had driven miles and miles to a lonely beach, pushing her car almost beyond its capacity, exceeding all speed limits, and had walked furiously for more than an hour, stumbling on the loose shingle. On the way back he had run out of petrol in the middle of nowhere, the fuel gauge on Chloe's car being notoriously unreliable, had felt even more foolish and angry with himself, had walked along the empty road until at last a pick-up truck passed which he was able to flag down. The kindness of its occupants – who not only took him to the only filling station in the vicinity but then drove him back to his car – eased his feelings slightly and he made his way home at a more sensible speed. (They had even intervened, with some incomprehensible haggling, over the deposit to be paid on the petrol-can; though, as Robert thought with chagrin, on the scale of expenses a petrol-can certainly costs a lot less than a Russian girl.) The back of the pick-up truck in which he'd travelled had been used to transport half-a-dozen goats a couple of hours earlier; Robert had a bath before going to bed.

A few days later Chloe gave him a basket and said, 'While you're weeding, pick the tips of the stinging nettles and we'll have them with rice for lunch.' She noted his expression and added, 'They're quite nourishing.'

'I've never eaten stinging nettles,' he admitted.

'There's always a first time for everything,' she said firmly.

His feelings still a little sore, Robert picked the nettles without gloves and felt obscurely that the tingling stings on his hands were a penance – though for what he would have been unable to say. While weeding he disturbed a toad (mating complete now, the surviving females – wide-eyed with concentration – having laid their strings of spawn); it slowly swelled to twice its normal size and gazed at him impassively.

A smell of death and rotting carrion that mingled from time to time with the sweeter smells of spring made him wonder if some other cat lay dead and awaiting burial. He investigated the furthest, wildest corner of the garden, spade in hand, and tracked down the smell to a group of tall, evil-looking arums with mottled, snakeskin stems, undulating deep red spathes and monstrous, stiff, upstanding dark purple-black spadices. A creeping of the spine, a sense that he was not alone: yet when he turned there was no one immediately behind him, just Chloe approaching a few yards off.

'They're rather magnificent, aren't they, even if they do smell quite foul,' she said as she disentangled her shawl from a briar and came up to him.

'You did warn me that not everything in your garden was very polite.' (This pleased her.) 'Actually, I imagined that I was going to have to bury something.'

'No, in this case it's life not death that stinks. The desire to perpetuate the species. Presumably the flies that fumble them find it irresistibly attractive – for of course a plant like that would never choose anything as innocent as bees or butterflies for its pollination partner.'

Robert held back the branches of the briar for Chloe to pass as they retreated towards more fragrant parts of the garden. 'When I die,' she said in ordinary conversational tones, 'what I would really like is to be buried here in the garden. I don't suppose the Church would allow it though.' She perched on the edge of the cistern. 'By the way,' she added, 'for reasons that I really don't think I need to explain, that arum was always held to be sacred to Priapus.' She smiled quite cheerfully. Then, 'Never mind,' she said – which since Chloe's conversation tended to zigzag backwards and forwards might have referred to the Church's intransigence, although Robert interpreted it personally and cleared his throat awkwardly.

The faint, far-off sound of mocking laughter.

When Jeremy next visited them she asked, 'By the way, where is your father buried?'

'He isn't,' replied Jeremy, 'he was cremated and we threw his ashes into the sea.'

*   *   *

'An island,' wrote Chloe three days later (having reflected on Jeremy's words), 'is surrounded by sea.' The absurdity of this statement annoyed her so that for a moment she considered crossing it out. Instead she expanded the thought: 'This is obvious, of course, but what it means is that an island lies open on all sides to whatever flotsam and jetsam the sea may cast up. It is true that the Mediterranean has the narrowest of entrances, yet in time anything thrown into the sea anywhere in the world might be carried through the Straits of Gibraltar, might perhaps one day be washed up on the shores of this island. Birds are sometimes blown off course by winter gales: who knows if something similar might not happen to fish, sent astray by strange underwater tides or currents? Who knows what a fish might have eaten? In fairy-tales a ring lost in the sea may be swallowed by a fish and opportunely found in its belly when the fish is served up at table.' (This last written with a small, sad smile; none of Chloe's rings had found its way into the sea.)

She stopped writing, picked up the Prayer Book, turned its pages until she found the right passage and read: *We therefore commit his body to the deep, to be turned into corruption, looking for the resurrection of the body (when the Sea shall give up her dead)* . . . Recently she had taken to reading aloud sometimes.

Robert noticed the increased frequency with which they ate fish, but assumed that this had something to do with Lent. He had found the stinging nettles on the whole rather disappointing though he was relieved at least that their after-effects were not as bad as he'd feared (for Chloe, having served him a large helping, had waited until he had finished eating it before announcing with a deceptively gentle smile which he felt might conceal a touch of mockery, 'They're a very powerful diuretic, you know').

* * *

However, in the end the nettles indirectly proved useful. As he explained to Anthony, 'It's a question of making something frightening and yet not *too* frightening – the drawing has got to be scary enough to thrill but not so terrifying that it produces nightmares.' Robert was illustrating a story about a dragon whose author had attempted to defuse the power of this large, scaly monster by making it a vegetarian; he had thus depicted it chewing furiously on a large mouthful of virulent-looking stinging nettles. 'Nettles make you pee actually,' he told Anthony, 'but I don't think I'd better draw that part of it.' ('Dragon's piss' thereafter passed into Anthony's vocabulary to denote artistic honesty.)

But dragons and fairy-tale monsters are not the most frightening things. Children tucked up safe in bed may shiver in delighted horror at these beings from another world (or, of course, may feel anxious when the light is turned off and have bad dreams), yet what is truly terrifying – in later years too – is more closely associated with everyday life: the sudden transformation of the familiar into the unfamiliar, the realisation that what you thought you knew has become alien, the face of the person you took for granted and trusted now menacing.

Chloe, who knew this, had never spoken or written of it. When the conversation turned to monsters one Sunday lunchtime (Jeremy having spoken of his father's great fondness for all the large monitor lizards but especially for the lumbering, flesh-eating Komodo dragons), she diverted her thoughts firmly from other kinds of threat into a reflection on the scaly embrace of a dragon. What this led her to say was, 'In Greek the word "dragon" is used for a serial rapist' (at which for some reason they both laughed and only she apparently thought of the victims' terror).

'Luckily my dragon isn't quite so bad,' said Robert, and –

unusually for him – went and fetched his folder of drawings to show them.

'By the way,' she added a little while later, 'while we're on the subject, that plant which shocked you so much in the garden, Robert, is commonly called the "dragon arum".' Jeremy was curious. Robert protested that nothing in her garden had ever shocked him, and received a strange look in return.

After watching the vipers mating, Chloe is curious. 'Do snakes have penises,' she asks him one day, 'and if so, where?' 'Indeed they do,' he answers, 'though except when needed they are kept inside the body. As a matter of fact, snakes and lizards have not one but two penises – not una est in their case.' She expresses disbelief, rebukes him for not being serious. 'I'm absolutely serious,' he says. 'They're called "hemipenes", which actually is rather a misnomer since they're not the two halves of one whole but are perfectly complete and functioning penises in their own right. Not both at the same time or serially,' he adds, 'it's simply a question of one or the other, not one after the other.' 'But why?' she asks. 'I imagine it's got something to do with the fact that in snakes and lizards copulation is rather complicated, he has to lift her tail with his tail to get at the right bit of her, probably having one penis on either side means that he can manage comfortably whichever side he approaches her from.' 'It doesn't sound very economical to me,' she comments. 'Oh well, I dare say there are some areas in life where one shouldn't economise,' says Robin cheerfully. This is a more or less public conversation at breakfast on the terrace; as they smile at each other a shadow falls over the table. Her husband. 'Robin has been telling me such interesting things about reptiles,' she says coolly as she pours the coffee, making it sound as if the subject bored her.

*   *   *

The following day, when they are alone, he says, 'I forgot to tell you that when a snake gets an erection its penis turns inside out.' It is not a moment for asking why. In years to come she remembers and wonders about it.

Someone else once told her quite a lot of interesting things about the brain. 'The reptile brain' was how he described the oldest part of the brain, responsible for the sense of smell, 'What used to be called the rhinencephalon.'

Chloe reflected that she would have to hold Jeremy naked in her arms to know whether he smelled like Robin. To Robert when he got back from driving Jeremy into town she said, 'He ought to have a girlfriend – someone of his own age, I mean.'

Robert was slightly surprised by this but merely answered, 'He probably does.' Apropos of another subject he had recently written to Annie, 'By now I really oughtn't to be surprised by anything that she says. I imagine it's probably because she's lived alone for so long that she sometimes seems to think aloud.' (A few nights previously he had heard Chloe apparently talking to herself as he passed her door on his way upstairs to bed.)

The reason that Robert was now regularly driving Jeremy back to town was that bus services to the village were few and far between on Sundays – and it had become accepted that Sunday was the day on which Jeremy came to lunch. ('I am a creature of habit,' declared Chloe, 'I like rituals.') Jeremy himself had said, 'You really don't have to, I can perfectly well walk down to the main road and hitch a lift,' but in fact Robert quite liked the drive and the opportunity to buy an English Saturday newspaper.

'Amazing,' was Jeremy's comment on the car as he watched Robert double-declutch at each change of gear, 'it must be a fair bit older than me.'

'It is. It's Chloe's,' said Robert.

'I'd realised that.'

'It still works though.' And Robert put his foot down on the accelerator.

'It's the first time I've ever been in a car that doesn't even *possess* seat-belts,' said Jeremy diplomatically.

'They're compulsory by law, but Chloe maintains that everyone knows her car and no one's going to fine her,' said Robert. He slowed down. 'At any rate, it's certainly true that no one has ever stopped me, though at the beginning I always used to feel nervous whenever I caught sight of a policeman.'

Jeremy invited Robert to have a coffee, thought of telling him about Robin, about Chloe, but in the end didn't.

Robert had of course made the connection and worked out that Jeremy's father was the author of the reptile book. He asked no questions.

'Who,' asked Anthony, 'is that remarkably *couth* young man I saw you hobnobbing with?'

'A friend of Chloe's. He's called Jeremy' (without knowing why, Robert omitted the surname).

'Ah.' (A pause.) 'Well, rather him than me keeping you company among those castrating old witches. As a matter of fact that black moustachioed one, the housekeeper, gave me a very funny look indeed in the market the other day, I had to put my hand into my trouser pocket and make an averting sign *instantly* – which considering that I was encumbered with shopping was rather awkward, it involved putting everything down, and I then got some funny looks of another kind, people probably thought I had a really impertinent itch that needed scratching, if not worse. All the same, much better be on the safe side, I swear that woman possesses the evil eye.'

Robert said nothing.

If Anthony noticed faint signs of discomfort he made no comment, merely pronouncing, 'Not only couth, but kempt into the bargain.'

'Leave it,' said Robert, 'you shouldn't be doing that, let me.' Chloe was balanced precariously on a ladder in the library, attempting to put a book away on the topmost shelf.

'I may be old but I am perfectly capable,' she said. (In snappish mode apparently.)

'Yes, but I'm taller.' Since this was patently true face was saved and she was able to accept his offer of help reasonably gracefully. She backed down the ladder, slowly and not quite steadily. Robert thought she was trembling slightly. He noted that at any rate the book was not about reptiles.

'I cannot stand mess,' she declared a trifle desperately.

It was not clear to him whether this referred only to books left lying around or to something else as well. Some felicitous inspiration made him respond mildly, 'But neither do you like petty-minded suburban neatness in the garden.'

Whereupon she relaxed and laughed. 'Oh dear, sorry, I apologise for that,' she said. 'But no, you're quite right, I don't. I like the garden wild and rampant and I like knowing that its ability to grow and flourish owes nothing to me or to anything that I might or might not do.' She added, 'From that point of view spring is a very salutary season for gardeners.'

In March they had lunch on the terrace for the first time and Robert idly watched a slim brown lizard sunning itself. For spring is the time of year when snakes and lizards, recently emerged from hibernation, need every bit of warmth they can find. Reptiles cannot eat or digest until their metabolic rate has reached a certain level. (Unfortunately for them, the black asphalt surface of the road absorbs heat and thus seems a promising source of life-giving energy, which is why Robert had recently been noticing the squashed remains of quite a few small reptiles.)

When you awake from hibernation, thought Chloe, the readjustment must be quite a shock. She shivered in the sunlight. 'When you are old,' she told Robert, 'you tend to feel the cold. I suppose you could say there's a sort of *impoverishment* about old age and among the other things that wear thin and threadbare is your insulation.'

He went and fetched her shawl, which she accepted a tiny bit ungraciously, making him feel clumsy. Then apologised: 'Sorry. That was kind of you, thank you.'

Advances and retreats.

Spring is also the season when young gods flourish then die, and indeed the time of year in which Chloe tended to meditate on such matters. The book Robert had put back in its place for her was *The Golden Bough*.

11

Robert dreamed that there was a Komodo dragon in the garden of his childhood, right at the back, by the wall. It was about three metres long, thickset and scaly. He knew that a small fair-haired boy entrusted to his care was playing under the apple tree; he sprinted out, scooped him up and ran back in, then remembered the cat, washing itself in the sun, ran out, grabbed it, then back into the safety of the house. He slammed the door, turned the key in the lock and slid the bolts into place. Relief. Suddenly, out of nowhere, there was a crowd of old people in the garden, twenty of them or more, men and women, shabby and shivering and threadbare. They were beating on the door in terror, begging him to open it and let them in. Robert powerfully, utterly, absolutely did not want to open the door. The Komodo dragon was approaching the house slowly, its nostrils questing, scenting. The old people were wailing and moaning. Robert knew that he had no choice. He opened the door and bundled them in, stumbling, falling over each other. They smelt of poverty. They were too frightened to speak. With a fraction of a second to spare as the dragon lumbered forward, Robert managed to get the door shut, locked and bolted. He stood with his back against it, panting.

He woke up, thought for a second that he could still hear the lizard's stertorous breathing, realised it was his own. He turned on the light, sat up, repeated to himself aloud three times 'I managed' – this being Annie's remedy for nightmares. ('If you didn't actually get *killed* in the dream or anything like that, just say to yourself firmly, "Yes, it was really bad but I managed to survive or to cope or whatever," then you'll probably be able to go back to sleep again.') In spite of the fact that she never wanted to hear what his nightmares were about, maintaining that dreams recounted are invariably lifeless and boring since they lack the essential dimension that makes them real for the dreamer, Annie was usually comforting. It is in any case easier to get back to sleep if there is someone warm and snoring faintly beside you, against whose familiar-smelling body you can lie close for reassurance. 'I managed to let them in, I did manage to open the door,' said Robert to himself once more (not, interestingly enough, 'I managed to shut the door'), yet knew that he would not be able to sleep now. He looked at his watch: almost five o'clock. He put on his dressing-gown and made his way down to the kitchen, trying hard to avoid the bits of the stairs that creaked.

However, he needn't have worried about waking Chloe for he found her sitting at the kitchen table. She showed no surprise at seeing him, merely putting aside what looked like a child's exercise book and saying, 'Hello, Robert, bring another cup and have some tea.'

He didn't feel capable of much conversation, nor did she appear to require it. Apart from one brief exchange they thus sat in companionable silence, drinking strong black tea as the first cocks crowed and the sky gradually lightened. And this in its own way was curiously comforting to both of them.

Chloe had stopped dreaming well nigh forty years before – or at any rate had stopped being aware of her dream world. Her sleeping patterns were becoming increasingly erratic, though this was not something that bothered her particularly; she would have agreed with what Annie had once told Robert, namely that insomnia only matters if you think it does, this having been said at a time, not long after he moved in with her, when his wife was divorcing him and he was more than usually fraught with anxiety.

(Anthony had once described Robert's wife – though not in front of Robert – as having a tight little give-nothing arse and a bossy bosom. 'A bad mixture,' he had pronounced, 'especially when combined with the fact that she's got far too many frightfully *glittering* teeth in that hygienic little mouth of hers.')

During her intervals of wakefulness Chloe sometimes read, more often wrote, or simply wandered among her own thoughts. She also of course wandered round the house from time to time. When you have lived in the same house for more than fifty years it becomes so intimately known that you can find your way around it in the dark; Chloe was familiar with every individual creak of stairs or wooden floors, rarely put on lights, even felt sometimes that in the stillness of the night the house breathed and sighed like a gentle and friendly animal.

What she had been thinking about when Robert appeared in the kitchen doorway in his dressing-gown was embraces. What she had just written was this:

'There are words which are simply plain matter-of-fact names for things, like "tree" or "stone". Or like "earring" and "pearl". Sometimes, as with "pearl", they may also have metaphorical meanings' (here Chloe couldn't help thinking of a pearl thrown away, richer than all his tribe), 'yet effectively the words carry one defined and specific meaning. Other words are more powerful, for what they encompass is not so much a single meaning as a conception or idea. "Lap" is a good such word: lying in the lap of luxury, lapped in languorous silks and velvets, lady, shall I lie in your lap . . . Lap encircles and enfolds. These idea-words probably exist in all languages. Perhaps they are the most important words. In Latin *sinus* expresses convexity as well as concavity, it is a word not only for hollow things – the secret empty spaces behind your cheek bones for example – but also denotes round things, curved things – a bay, a bosom. In Greek *kolpos* is similarly a word for encompassment; as well as meaning bay it is also vagina.' Chloe laid her pen down at this point and thought of breasts and vaginas and encircling, of arms and legs. She thought of land-locked bays. 'The earth,' she wrote, 'could be said to embrace the sea and all that might be within it. The sea lies in the lap of the earth.'

To Robert she said reflectively, 'I think I rather like words that begin with "l".'

This was no odder than anything else in that quiet, early morning kitchen. He said the first word that came to mind: 'Liquidambar' (perhaps this came from Annie).

'Yes,' she said, 'and liquefaction.'

They were silent once more.

Lewdness, lust, lubricity, libidinousness, lasciviousness, longing. And love, of course.

An impartial observer might have noted two things about the progression of Chloe's notebooks. First, during the last few months she had been writing less of the garden and more of other, apparently disconnected, subjects. Second, her handwriting had recently undergone another subtle change: the firm, large, confident hand that had replaced her earlier tiny pinprick writing had in turn evolved into something freer and wilder, her letters more loosely looped and curled.

*   *   *

At lunch that day Chloe was upright and unbending and – if Robert understood right – commented to Maria with some acerbity that artichokes would make a pleasant change from beans. After dinner, though, when Robert showed her the garnet earrings he had bought for Annie, she poured some more wine for both of them, ran her finger round the neck of the decanter with its flashing firelit diamond, and told him, 'I always used to wear pearls. However, I stopped wearing earrings so long ago that my ears arc no longer pierced even – the holes have quite closed up.'

A pause: nothing further was apparently forthcoming.

'Pearls must have looked good on you, Chloe,' said Robert politely.

'It's rather complicated,' he tells her, 'but it's certainly not true, as many people believe, that they don't have ears.'

Annie liked the earrings. For a few brief seconds it crossed her mind that unexpected presents are sometimes guilt offerings; this thought seemed unworthy though, so she dismissed it firmly and telephoned Robert to thank him. He sounded more relaxed, less hesitant than usual. An hour later Annie was extremely rude to a client and thus lost an important piece of work.

'Geckos' ears are particularly interesting. In fact they've got a rather better auditory apparatus than most lizards – which is what you might expect, considering the way they vocalise.' Polite conversation over lamp-lit dinner on the terrace. Chloe has always liked the squeaking geckos, seeing them as small, benign house spirits. 'Snakes are a different matter, they have no ear drums yet at low frequencies they can hear better than cats do.' Chloe has always liked his young and earnest seriousness. 'A young man with a passion for snakes and

lizards,' wrote the friend who first proposed that he stay with them; 'Please make it quite clear to him that I don't want any snakes introduced into my house,' said Michalis.

No serpents in my garden. But then, 'My wife has green fingers,' he had said, and of course, right from the beginning, it had always been her garden.

'Poor woman, I think she did not always have an easy life,' said Jeremy's landlady on learning where he went to lunch each Sunday.

Jeremy, who had been wondering how to find out more, had a sudden flash of intuition that asking questions would be counterproductive and thus merely commented in neutral tones, 'It's a beautiful place.'

'Yes,' said his landlady, who had never been inside the gates. 'My father worked there,' she added. (She was a big woman, and her father had also been a big, well-built man.)

'My father stayed there once.'

'He must have been a very young man then, because afterwards they did not ever have visitors.'

By mutual and tacit agreement their conversation ended here. Reciprocity oils the works of human relations: Jeremy liked to practise his beginner's Greek with his landlady and she, who over the years had learnt fairly good English from her tenants, liked in turn to practise this with him (and perhaps to show off a tiny bit). Reciprocal curiosity also tends to be productive, and the landlady, having rapidly reckoned dates and ages and wondering how much – if anything – Jeremy knew, determined to do a bit of discreet fishing at some point in the near future.

After Robin's departure Michalis killed any snake he came across with an excess of concentrated violence that horrified Chloe.

*   *   *

'So unlike the home life of our dear Queen,' pronounced Anthony, 'more like the House of Usher.' Then, in a moment of honesty, 'Actually, to tell you the truth, I've no idea what the House of Usher is or was.'

'It's a story by Edgar Allan Poe, I think.'

'Have you read it?'

'No,' said Robert.

'Oh dear, neither have I. But anyway, I'm quite sure that Madame Chloe's life must have been more like something out of Poe than something out of Balmoral. Too much sex for Scotland, for a start.'

Robin's pockets or his canvas bag are often full of stones whose colour or shape or markings have pleased him. Now he reaches across to his bag and extracts an almost spherical dull black marble pebble found on a beach, the size of a large pea. He thinks it goes with the black pearls in her ears. He places it in her navel and says, 'This is an exercise in concentration: you are going to keep so still and I am going to be so gentle that this stone will not be dislodged.' It does not work though. Exercises in harmony.

Sunlight and the song of birds. In winter Robert had balanced on a ladder and pruned the wisteria that grew up the house and threatened to weave its way across Chloe's bedroom window ('Cut it back to two buds please, Robert, yes, there, like that, don't be afraid to be ruthless for once'); now it was beginning to flower. For the dominant colours of the springtime countryside are yellows and fresh, young greens, yet in Chloe's garden Judas trees, lilac and wisteria added pinks and tender mauves. Colours of aching innocence and sweetness, reborn each year. A harmony of a different kind.

*   *   *

Robert wrote to Annie about these colours, wrote too of the asphodel that was flowering so profusely over the hillsides. 'The best word to describe its colour,' he wrote, 'is *vanilla* – a sort of warm browny white with a touch of pink in it.'

Annie, who had always felt that there is romance in the names of certain trees and flowers, had once told him that 'asphodel' is the most magic name of all; when she got his letter she thought he must have remembered this. She considered telephoning him but didn't. Instead she rang Hetty, with whom she had a silly, petty argument which made her feel miserable. That evening she had a minor car accident in which luckily no one was hurt but which left her fairly shaken. Having always maintained stoutly that women make much better drivers than men, she felt reluctant to mention it to Robert.

'Asphodel,' said Chloe at lunch time (having thanked him for the large bunch of it that he had picked), 'is what Persephone was picking when Pluto raped her. You seem to have survived the experience intact, Robert.' (He cleared his throat.) 'It is also what grew in the Elysian fields. Pliny saw it from a much more mundane point of view though and said that it repels mice and rats, which personally I very much doubt.'

Chloe had in fact been thinking recently of the frog and mouse imagery and deciding that she didn't much like it: 'Cool and wet and insolent as opposed to warm and furry and timid is not right at all,' she concluded to herself. 'All the same,' she mused, 'I seem to remember that the frog who would a-wooing go was courting someone called Mistress Mouse.' For a moment she suddenly wondered if she had spoken aloud but since Robert didn't react presumed that the thought had remained in her own head.

He was getting up from the table, thanking her politely for

the meal. What she said out loud was, 'Robert, do you have a girlfriend?'

This was disingenuous, for quite apart from the fact that the garnet earrings implied the existence of such a person (although Robert had reticently described them as 'a present for a friend'), Chloe was of course familiar with the content of some of Annie's letters to him; indeed, the train of thought which led her to ask him this question had to do with something private that she had read in one of these letters. It occurred to her that the word 'girlfriend' was not perhaps quite suitable – but then 'mistress' wouldn't do either, would be even worse.

In any case he didn't dispute the word, though he dropped his napkin on the floor and stooped his shoulders slightly in a way that Chloe had come to recognise meant awkwardness or discomfort.

He answered, 'Yes, I mean, mmm, well, as a matter of fact, yes.'

'Perhaps you might wish to invite her to spend a few days here, you might like her to come and visit you for Easter, let us say, if she is free.'

A pause. 'Do you really mean that, Chloe?'

Sharpness. 'I am not in the habit of saying what I do not mean.' (I mean what I say is the same as I say what I mean. Or is it?) 'You may prefer to think about it, Robert, and let me know in due course.'

New ideas take a bit of getting used to.

There was never anything in the least insolent, there was never any timidity. He always managed quite comfortably whichever side he approached me from.

People's small personal possessions are imbued with a kind of mana that makes them, when their owners die, intensely valuable to those who survive. 'Mementoes' is not the right word, for it is not simply a matter of remembering: these objects work on a level more closely akin to magic, they provide a link, a continuity of relation, an abiding contact with someone once loved. Perhaps in some ways they have something in common with a child's comfort objects.

Jeremy was extremely attached to the somewhat battered canvas shoulder-bag in which he carried books and notebooks.

'It used to belong to my father,' he told Robert, 'he always had it, as far back as I can remember. It's quite immortal, they made things to last in those days, though the strap's been repaired a couple of times.' He added, smiling at the recollection, 'When I was a child I used to call it his "Jeremy Fisher bag" because I thought it was like the fishing satchel in the Beatrix Potter story. I sort of identified with Jeremy Fisher actually, I suppose children always like characters who have the same name as their own.'

'Yes,' said Robert, thinking with a twinge of retrospective embarrassment of Rob Roy and Robert the Bruce and various other fictional or historical swashbuckling heroes.

Chloe in the past couple of days had also been thinking from time to time of Robert in his dressing-gown, looking a bit tense as he sat at the kitchen table with both hands round his cup of tea as if he was seeking warmth. The shabbiness of the old towelling dressing-gown was somehow endearing. (Anthony, trying very hard to be tactful when Robert had arrived to stay with him, had controlled the first remarks that came to mind and had merely said, 'It does rather look as if it's seen better days,' then, observing on his friend's face the expression that he privately called 'Robbie's little sulk of obstinacy', had refrained from further comment.) Something else that had pleased Chloe was the fact that under this garment Robert appeared to be wearing an even older, faded T-shirt; she was unable to see what – if anything – he wore below the waist since he kept the folds of the dressing-gown closely wrapped. (Actually a perfectly decent navy-blue pair of what Robert called 'pants' and Annie 'knickers', though the chain-store that sold them labelled them 'briefs'.)

Two Christmases earlier, Annie had given Robert a rather expensive and beautiful silk dressing-gown – 'silk lined with silk, to be warmer'. Shortly after he started working for Chloe she had written, 'By the way, you forgot to take your dressing-gown.' 'I know,' Robert might have replied, but tactfully didn't.

There is something familiar and friendly about sitting unselfconsciously together in your oldest nightclothes.

Mementoes or small objects impregnated with magic power: it is hard to throw them away, though sometimes you wonder why. Even if you never look at them, you always know they are there. Among the things that Chloe kept in an old wooden cigar box by her bed was a pyjama button.

He wears cotton pyjamas of a classical, striped variety. This she knows for she has seen them on the washing line: they have three buttons on the jacket, a cord around the waist and – surprisingly, as it seems to her – three more chaste buttons at the flies. She knows him clothed and she knows him naked but these pyjamas belong to a private part of his life, these are what he wears when he sleeps and dreams alone. Once she goes to the laundry basket when no one is around and ransacks it, finds his pyjamas, clutches them, caresses them, holds them to her face and breathes in the scent of his sleeping body. 'I am jealous of his pyjamas,' she thinks. But this is a kind of madness. She does not do it again.

*   *   *

The green-eyed monster.

The truth is that jealousy lives on even when the ability to speak of it is gone. 'Insanity only matters if you think it does,' Chloe was later to say to herself rather desperately. Nevertheless she decided to employ a big, heavily built man to sleep in the house at night.

12

Robert was impatient with Anthony.

'You make all these things up,' he protested, 'there's not a shred of truth in any of it.'

'Everyone knows that she grows strange plants in her garden – fleabane, henbane, ratsbane and no doubt worse. Deadly nightshade probably. Hemlock. Anyway, I have my sources. People *remember* things, you know.'

'Well, in that case people quite simply remember things wrong.' (Robert, curiously offended at the suggestion that Chloe had resorted to herbal means of abortion rather than bear her husband any children, was categorical.)

'Don't be frightened,' said Chloe, 'it's not poisonous.'

'I know,' said Jeremy.

A forked tongue flickering. A long, dark snake lying loosely coiled in the spring sunlight, alert but unalarmed.

'Perhaps you know what it is then' (a challenge maybe).

'*Elaphe longissima*.' (Jeremy was not above a little showing off.) 'It's the snake of Asklepios.'

'I give them all a wide berth,' admitted Robert, who by now had encountered two or three snakes in the garden and had never been able to repress that instant of alarm, the sudden gasp, the leap of the heart in horror.

'Oh,' said Jeremy lightly, 'they're only frightening if you think they are. They're the lords of life, or so my father used to maintain. He liked that phrase – it's from a poem he always quoted, though who wrote it escapes me, I'm afraid.'

Chloe was rather silent at lunch. Jeremy felt for some reason that it might be better not to stay too long and thus, pleading work to be completed, asked Robert if he'd mind taking him back to town a bit earlier than usual. After they left Chloe wandered out into the garden once more; the sun was lower in the sky now, the stones where the snake had basked beneath the white oleander lay in deep shadow, the snake itself long since retired into some secret fissure. Birdsong and memories only. A chilliness.

The idea that memories might be mistaken is hard to bear. For if memories are wrong, then experience may no longer be valid: if one detail is flawed, how can you rely on the integrity of the whole, how can you be sure of anything? Are 'life' and 'creation' interchangeable?

In theological terms perhaps they are, thought Chloe sadly.

That night she did not change for dinner.

(Her evening clothes had surprised Robert at the beginning, for whereas most women who change for dinner put on a dress, Chloe did the opposite: she wore a dress or skirt during the day but in the evenings invariably made her appearance in a pair of black trousers and tunic of some kind.)

'Please go ahead and eat, Robert,' she said, serving him. 'I shall have a glass of wine to keep you company.'

'Look' (after a moment's hesitation) 'I don't want to fuss but . . .'

'I am quite all right. I am simply not hungry.' And a minute or so later: 'I have an ache, that is all.'

Robert put down his knife and fork. 'Perhaps you should call a doctor, Chloe, I could take you into town now if you wanted, if you're not feeling well it might be a good idea . . .'

'It's not that sort of ache,' she said firmly, 'I don't need a doctor. Your food is getting cold, do eat it.'

There is sometimes something faintly awkward about being the only person at table eating: every mouthful seems to take longer than usual to chew and your knife and fork make an unconscionable clatter on your plate. Robert refused a second helping.

'There is a sort of homoeopathic principle,' declared Chloe, 'by which a small ache cures a larger one. It's similar to the use of snake venom as an antidote to snake bite.'

She seemed to consider this an adequate explanation. Robert felt unsure and wondered what – if anything – he should do. He remembered the words of a friend of Annie's who shared the care of an elderly relative and always referred to her couple of evenings a week as 'babysitting'. 'It's a terrible responsibility when they're so old,' she had said.

Annie herself always knew what to do. When Hetty at the age of three and a half had cut her head quite badly Annie had simply wrapped her in a blanket and driven her to the nearest hospital. This she had once told Robert when they were comparing their worst experiences: 'Oh God, Robert, we had to wait for what seemed like ages, there was blood everywhere, it was quite *awful*, and Hetty bawling non-stop. When finally our turn came and a doctor saw us he took one look and said, "It's all right, Mother, no need to panic." Of course, if I'd thought about it I suppose I should have realised that the fact that she was bawling was a good sign . . .' As an afterthought she'd added, 'I was so relieved that Hetty was going to survive that I just meekly put up with being addressed as "Mother" in that condescending way.'

On this occasion Robert had only told Annie his second

worst experience; it was not until quite a bit later that he managed to tell someone the very worst thing of all. (The two were connected.)

Head wounds bleed profusely.

'Anyway, I don't much like doctors,' Chloe concluded, sounding perfectly brisk and normal, 'so I don't have one. What's more, when you're my age, Robert, strange young doctors tend to assume you're in your second childhood. When I last saw one a couple of years ago he addressed me in a loud voice as "Granny" – I dare say he thought it sounded kindly or something, but personally I found it intolerable. As a matter of fact' (very decidedly) 'I have never had any problems whatsoever with my hearing.'

Dearly beloved, know this, that the Almighty God is the Lord of life and death and of all things to them pertaining, as youth, strength, health, age, weakness and sickness. 'That,' said Chloe to herself as she read these words that night, 'would seem to cover it all. No doctor could possibly compete.'

However, these are simply means of trying to refocus one's thoughts. The difference made by a single noun: lords of life or lords of creation. *The Lord of life.* A faltering of confidence, an ache of uncertainty: Chloe opened her cigar box – redolent of the tobacco of half a century earlier – and scrutinised its diverse contents. *Break not the bruised reed, nor quench the smoking flax,* she read a little while later, but was not much comforted by thoughts of the reed-bed, of youth and strength.

'Tell me something useful for a change,' demanded Robert, 'tell me the name of a good doctor. And preferably one who speaks English.'

Instant solicitude. 'Oh Robert, is something the matter, aren't you feeling well? *Of course* we'll find you a good doctor, but hadn't you better tell me what kind you need?' (No immediate response.) 'Robbie, you don't have to be shy, even if it's something terribly embarrassing, I'm quite capable of being discreet, do please tell me what's the matter.'

'Nothing's the matter, I'm fine, I'm perfectly all right, there's no need to fuss. It simply seemed a good idea to know the name of a doctor and I remembered the man who came to see you when you had bronchitis' (Robert had let him in). 'He looked pleasant enough.'

Anthony eyed him doubtfully.

Robert, whose powers of invention suddenly failed him, added rather lamely, 'Just in case I got bitten by a snake in the garden or something.'

'I'm by no means certain how much he knows about poisonous snakes but he *is* quite nice and unjudgmental, which always helps. Anyway, I'll give you his name and number. Here,' said Anthony, writing them on the back of an old envelope. He added, 'I must say, you do *look* well, in fact if appearances are anything to go by you've been looking indecently healthy recently. Must be all that fresh air or Chloe's herbal brews. All the same, are you really *certain* you're not ill?'

'Yes,' said Robert.

'By the way,' Anthony remarked much more cheerfully a quarter of an hour later, as Robert got up to leave, 'I'm not sure what the man's English is like but you can always point to the offending member.'

In the garden at twilight he comments that all the white flowers are innocent and luminous. They are standing by the white oleander. Chloe has already changed for the evening into a flowing dress whose paleness also stands out in the darkening garden. A faint scent of gardenia in her hair. 'They are not always so innocent,' she says, 'an infusion of oleander has long been used locally as an abortifacient – it's so poisonous that the baby invariably dies, the only problem for all the poor village girls who resort to it in terror and desperation being that the mother often dies as well. And as for that one' (pointing to the datura whose pendent white flowers are so sweetly scented in the evening air) 'someone – though I can't remember who – says that a small dose makes you hallucinate, a larger dose drives you irrevocably mad, and an even larger dose kills you – only of course I don't know what the doses are.' She is tense and ill at ease, knowing that in a few minutes they must put on their public manners and appear on the terrace for dinner. 'Hush,' Robin says, then again, 'hush, listen to the bats.' She cannot bear to tell him that for the past year or so she has no longer been able to hear such high frequencies. He leads her discreetly behind the datura bush, puts his arms around her, holds her close, 'Chloe, Chloe,' he says and kisses her.

In the hospital someone had once called her 'Chloe', had said, 'You don't mind me calling you Chloe, do you,' as if this were a statement rather than a question, had apparently not heard her say, 'Yes I do actually, I object very strongly.' 'But,' as she afterwards thought, 'perhaps I never did say it out loud.' Often silence is the least painful way.

Afterwards, of course, there was plenty of time for reflecting on all the things that were never said, never even thought of. 'Did it really never occur to us that I might get pregnant? And why not?' she wondered. This puzzle haunted her for a while until she laid it to rest: 'It was because everything was outside time and place,' she decided. Later a further question came to torment her: why was it only at the very end that she conceived? But with the passing of the years she ceased to seek an explanation.

To Robert she thought of saying, 'The body seeks to remember, it is memories that ache in body and mind,' yet was silent.

What she did say (in spite of herself) was, 'Can you still hear bats squeak, Robert?'

He paused to think. 'Do you know,' he answered finally, 'I don't think I can. I used to, but I can't remember having heard them since I've been here.'

For a moment she looked so sad that he felt – quite inexplicably – an impulse to touch her; had it been evening he might have reached out across the table and laid his hand on hers, for example. However, such a presumption seemed quite out of place at lunch, so he merely smiled and felt awkward.

Chloe thought that Robert's rather hesitant smile made him look suddenly younger.

The moment passed.

The awkward, jarring feelings that can never be denied are hurt, anger, jealousy, pain: of these there can be no doubt.

Jealousy is an ugly one: not poppy, nor mandragora, nor all the drowsy syrups of the world, shall ever medicine thee to that sweet sleep which thou ow'dst yesterday. These were late night thoughts, in themselves not conducive to sleep.

'Get rid of as much of that horrible Bermuda clover as you can, but don't weed out the seedlings with the rather glaucous leaves, they're opium poppies,' she told him; this was a couple of mornings later as they inspected the further reaches of the garden. 'They used to grow on the roadside outside the gate, but people are so paranoid about narcotics that the local council put paid to them with an overdose of weedkiller. I dare say they were afraid the police might turn up and accuse everyone of drug-dealing or something. However, luckily by then the poppies had already seeded themselves into the garden, and thank goodness no one ever comes in here to see what I grow or don't grow. I'm very fond of all poppies, but specially these – they are a wonderful shade of dark, smoky pink, as you will see before too long.'

'Fine,' said Robert. He had noticed a flourishing patch of cannabis plants the previous summer, had wondered but had said nothing, had simply watered them dutifully.

Chloe (in another of her little flashes of telepathy perhaps) said, 'There are a great many plants in this garden that some people might not approve of. The cannabis, incidentally, originally came from birdseed. I don't have any use for it myself these days but if you wanted to harvest some you could.'

Robert mumbled something along the lines of, 'I won't, but thank you.'

'That young German used to help himself,' she added, 'without even so much as a by your leave – but I thought as long as he wasn't too greedy I'd turn a blind eye.'

More than once she had thought that if you really wanted to commit suicide there were a great many means at hand in the garden which would involve no bloodshed. You could make an infusion of hemlock and drink it, for example, after sacrificing a white cock to Asklepios. (Blood shed in sacrifice does not count.)

Inward-holding or outward-moving: perhaps there is a sort of sexual differentiation in methods of suicide. Women may take poison, men may shoot themselves.

However, the weight of people's disapproval is something that simply has to be borne. Having always rather liked that primitive sensation of a clearly defined entity of *body* inside which one wakes each day, Chloe had never in the least wished to kill herself, not even in the worst moments.

In the worst moments, the best thing to do is to suspend *I am* and to concentrate on *it is*. The garden is a good place for doing so.

She had once written: 'People build and rebuild, so that it is not easy to say how old this house is. Certainly the vaulted cellar is the oldest part. The garden walls are, I suspect, almost as old, their original purpose no doubt having been protection for man and beast against a hostile world. The oldest thing in the garden, however, is the earth itself: a rich, dark, friable soil which bears mute witness to the centuries during which it has been cultivated and tended. For of course the house would have had no meaning or purpose – an empty shell – if the garden had not been there to provide food for its inhabitants. It is only during the last hundred and fifty years or so that a flower garden was gradually created here. Should I then have returned this land to its earlier purpose and devoted it to the cultivation of chick peas and beans, lentils and spinach and onions? I think not. For the very word *purpose* denotes a human frame of reference: plants have no purpose or conscience, they simply *are*.'

A further reflection: 'Being human, I am of course incapable of following this thought to its logical conclusion and leaving the earth to its own devices; I weed and water and adjudicate in the constant rivalries between rampant green growth. I compromise.'

During the past few months Chloe had been sitting at the table late at night and rereading her old notebooks. A new thought now came to mind as she pondered on the accuracy of memory: 'I have built and rebuilt so much that it is no longer quite clear how old I am.'

'I am too old for you,' she says. This is the realistic view, though her smile is perhaps an attempt to take the sting from it, to disarm reality. 'You are ageless,' he replies.

When Robert diffidently suggested planting a few tomatoes for the summer, Chloe said, 'Plants that are poisonous to human beings are often of great beauty. Which is probably why I grow more poisonous plants than edible plants these days.' She laughed. 'But, yes, go ahead with your tomatoes. In any case, it's all relative, they're one of the things that are both poisonous and edible.' Seeing him look puzzled, she explained, 'Like potatoes' (this didn't much illuminate him) 'vegetable alkaloids.'

Robert went into town that afternoon and succeeded in finding a dozen healthy-looking young tomato plants; he also bought envelopes, string, tea (for Chloe), as well as a rather indecent postcard that had caught his eye (for Anthony, who collected such things: 'Don't look so prudish and po-faced, Robert, they'll be collectors' items one day'). These days he tended to leave the car some distance from the market, beyond the ramparts, having found this to be a good parking place one Sunday when he drove Jeremy home. 'The coward's solution' was an uneasy thought.

'Realism' is a false refuge, a sensible-sounding word that covers a multitude of fears.

'It was in the end simply a failure of courage,' Chloe recognised. 'I did not dare and so I said I was too old.'

'Vivamus atque amemus,' he says, 'let us live and love. And

146

anyway, Catullus was twenty-two when he met his Lesbia.'
'Is that true,' she asks, 'or did you just make it up?' 'No,
it's perfectly true, the dates are well attested,' he replies.
'Not a very auspicious comparison.' 'Perhaps not, but you
know what I mean.' This is in the time when they are still
laughing.

You do not, of course, expect a young man of his age to live in
perfect chastity. She never asks him about his winter life and
he never tells her of it, not even later when so-called realities
are beginning to intrude.

Robert watched Chloe carefully over the next week or so. She
was aware of this but, curiously enough, found that she didn't
mind it. (She was unaware, of course, of the doctor's name
and telephone number tucked safely away in his wallet.) Her
appetite improved.

One evening she mused, 'People used to consider tomatoes
an aphrodisiac for some reason,' and only realised that she had
spoken aloud when Robert responded firmly, 'Well, I can't say
that I have ever found them to be so.'

'No,' she said, and then admitted, 'Oh dear, actually,
Robert, I didn't really mean to say that out loud, it was
only a passing thought.'

'No harm done,' he said, 'it's all right,' and both of them
felt quite comfortable about it.

13

All day long the bells had been tolling, the flag on the Town Hall at half-mast.

'Who's died?' asked Robert; he had come into town to buy an English newspaper but had not yet read it and in any case thought it unlikely that local Greek news would get much coverage; he had run into Anthony by chance and they were having a quick coffee together (rather too close to the market for comfort).

'Jesus,' said Anthony, and it took Robert a moment to realise that this was an answer rather than an imprecation.

'I usually walk,' said Chloe. (She had announced her intention of going to the village for the Good Friday service, whereupon Robert had offered to take her there in the car.) 'Perhaps you might walk with me, unless of course it would be a terrible bore for you.'

'No,' he said, 'I'd like to come.'

'Rituals please me, you see,' she explained as they set off just before twilight, 'and the death of a young god is the biggest ritual of all. I'm sorry, I don't think I can walk very fast.'

Robert, who had been trying to tailor his stride to suit hers, gave her his arm. This involved stooping slightly.

He had hesitated for ten days or so before asking Annie if she'd like to come out and visit him for Easter, one of the reasons for this being that the idea of juxtaposing Chloe and Annie provoked a certain amount of unease. (Robert recognised this himself, although he didn't quite understand why and in any case the recognition didn't help, left him if anything even less able to make up his mind.) In the end, as it happened, he found he'd delayed too long; when he finally telephoned Annie she told him that she'd already promised to house-sit for her brother and couldn't back out at the last minute.

Chloe accepted this news without comment.

'Never mind, such a pity that Western and Orthodox Easters coincide this year, but it just can't be helped,' was Annie's conclusion. Her usual matter-of-fact tone here, though when she added wistfully, 'I would have loved to see the asphodel in flower,' Robert felt that she was speaking of other things too; moreover, he thought he detected the faintest echo of a wail behind her composure and suddenly recalled a conversation about the power of words and the magic in names (completely forgotten when he'd written to her about the colour of asphodel), which strangely gave rise to a surge of desire for the *familiarity* of her.

Robert walked with Chloe, lighted tapers in their hands, at the back of the procession that bore the flower-bedecked bier of the dead god round the village. The elusive scent of the funereal mauve and white stocks, the flickering points of light as tapers guttered, their flames dipping in a sudden breeze then, courtesy of the hands that hastily sheltered them, growing steady once more. The dirge-like hymn, slow and repetitious.

'It is supposed,' whispered Chloe, 'to be the lament of the Virgin Mary for her dead son.' Robert thought she added, 'It is erotic,' and wondered if he had misheard.

You grieve over the death of a young man, the firm, sweet,

youthful flesh for ever stilled, a young god; you grieve over the death of a man who once was young. Ah my sweet springtime.

In spring the birds that return are swallows and swifts and cuckoos, and hoopoes who are the princes among birds. This she has told him and thinks that he has remembered it when he encloses a postcard for her in the polite letter asking if he may once more spend the summer with them: the card shows the fossilised remains of Archaeopteryx *and on it he has written, 'He was a prince of great beauty in his day.' To Chloe the imprint of his feathery wings in the mud of so many million years ago makes him look more like a fallen angel: an angel who came to grief, his head twisted back at a strange angle, his neck perhaps broken in that final plummet from the heavens to the mire.*

In spring the waiting grows impatient.

At lunch the previous week Chloe had listened to Robert and Jeremy arguing about the relative importance of word and image in the comic strip.

'They cheapen life,' she declared obstinately, 'they are crude and ugly.'

'A lot are,' admitted Robert, 'but to be fair some are really very accomplished within their own terms.' Chloe was not convinced. He tried to explain: 'It's a different convention.'

'What's more,' said Jeremy, 'you can't say that it isn't a convention with an impeccable pedigree. Think of ancient Greek vases – the sequence of scenes almost always has the names of the protagonists written over their heads so that you can identify the story depicted. And sometimes it's not just names, sometimes the words are clearly being spoken, the ancient equivalent of a speech-bubble.'

This interested Robert. 'Like what?' he asked.

'Well, for example there's a lovely vase showing a swallow flying in the sky and a man standing beneath it with the words "Spring, spring, the swallow has arrived" more or less issuing from his mouth.'

'Is that true,' asked Chloe sharply, 'or did you make it up?'

'No, it's true.'

'There are swallows and there are swifts and there are martins. This is not a swallow, it's a swift,' corrected Chloe automatically a couple of mornings later. ('There's a swallow in the pond,' he had said, suddenly spotting it.) Then, 'Oh dear, I haven't got a net, can you reach, Robert, and get it out before it drowns.'

The bird had flown too low over the water, in an attempt to drink perhaps, had in a fatal moment of miscalculation dipped a wingtip below the surface, and was now floating in the cistern, alive but waterlogged. Robert knelt on the parapet, found he couldn't reach, hesitated a few seconds then took off his shoes, stepped into the water fully clothed and retrieved it.

'Wait,' said Chloe and went to fetch some absorbent kitchen paper. 'It may die of shock and fear,' she told him as she took the swift from his hands and dried it gently as best she could. 'They can't take off from the ground, they're entirely aerial, they never land,' she added. 'Perhaps if we put it somewhere high up, in the sun so that it can warm up and dry off a bit more, it might have a chance.'

Being taller, Robert took the bird from her once more and placed it in the highest fork of the almond tree that he could reach. It weighed almost nothing in his hand: a tiny, motionless, frightened, frail morsel of life. I have never held a bird in my hands before, he thought.

What Chloe thought was: Not a sparrow falls . . . (she had

added the Bible to her night-time reading, though on the whole she tended to concentrate more on the Old Testament). What she said was, 'You'd better go and change at once, Robert. It would probably be a good idea to take those trousers off outside the kitchen door and give them to Maria to deal with, rather than dripping duckweed all the way up the stairs – there's no need to be modest, I imagine she's seen a man with his trousers off before now and I take it you're probably wearing something perfectly respectable underneath them.' After Robert had moved away it occurred to her that this had somehow been unkind, so that she called, 'Thank you for rescuing it,' but he did not turn round so probably was out of earshot.

'It was obviously what you might call a rather fraught relationship,' says Robin, 'but when her pet sparrow died she grieved and he wrote the tenderest of poems about it.' Chloe, who never cries, is not particularly moved at the thought of Catullus's mistress's red and swollen eyes.

In the afternoon Robert found the swift lying dead on the ground beneath the almond tree, the shock of plunging out of its own element clearly having been too great to withstand. He rather surprised himself by burying it instead of merely throwing it into the bushes. He felt reluctant to mention this death to Chloe; thus, when she asked whether he'd been to see how the bird was, answered cautiously, 'It doesn't seem to be there any more.' Chloe knew that he was lying, understood why, and asked nothing further.

After a while she said, 'I always wait for the swifts to return. They invariably take me by surprise, one day I suddenly hear a shrilling and I look up and they are there.'

It is important to be accurate. When you know something by its proper name, you can see its details more clearly. A swift is not a swallow, a frog is not a toad, a weasel is not a stoat, a rabbit is not a hare.

These thoughts made Chloe say that evening, 'Did you know that in Greek Peter Rabbit is called "Peter the Little Hare"?'

They had been speaking of birds and of the binoculars through which Chloe watched them ('The birdwatcher is a kind of voyeur,' she had noted calmly, 'if being a voyeur means looking from the outside in at something which is complete without you'). Robert did not of course understand the train of thought that had led her to Peter Rabbit but was quite glad to move off the subject of voyeurism; he had, as it happened, briefly considered taking his trousers off before getting into the pond but then for some obscure reason decided not to. In any case he was by now used to her conversational leaps and tangents, and thus responded quite easily, 'Well, Beatrix Potter must be turning in her grave then, if she'd wanted a hare she would certainly have drawn one.'

If one is to call things by their proper names, then adultery is always adultery. This much is simple.

'I concentrate on feeling,' she says, 'I turn my mind away from thought, that is why I do not say anything.' Later she reflects that it is rare to be able to cease thinking, that Robin's embrace was the only place where it was ever possible. A sense of utter simplicity. A time of silence. Robin's arms are strong and covered with blond hairs, Robin's armpits are young and ardent, the smell of his sweat fresh and tender, Robin's hands are shapely and accomplished. But this of course is thinking once more: the naming of parts.

The second worst experience in Robert's life had been coming home unexpectedly early and finding his wife in bed with a colleague of hers. Two feelings jostled in his mind, the first of which – It is *my* bed – found its way into words quite easily. The second feeling was harder to formulate though perhaps Chloe's words, spoken so much later, came near to expressing it: that what was taking place on Robert's bed was perfectly complete without him.

'It was so humiliatingly like the worst kind of cheap bedroom farce,' he said when he told Anthony about it. '*Of course* I should have known, but I didn't.'

These words were spoken some years after the event described, on a hot summer night shortly before Robert started working for Chloe as he and Anthony strolled through quiet back streets after a leisurely dinner.

'It was probably a blessing in disguise, Robert, look at it that way,' said Anthony. 'Silver linings and all that.'

Some time later, as Robert prepared for bed, he had a sudden thought and called through the half-open bathroom door, 'Actually, I suppose in a way you could say my marriage did leave me with one useful legacy – I did at least learn how to look after my teeth' (his ex-wife being a dentist).

Later still, in the moments before sleep came, Robert said to himself, 'If Annie ever had someone else, at least she wouldn't do it in our own bed' – but this was not, of course, an entirely consoling idea.

The thing that is hardest to forgive is humiliation.

'I will never forgive you' are words spoken in a variety of contexts.

She had laughed once, many years before, and had said lightly, 'If you shoot a swallow, then I'll never forgive you.' This was when Michalis complained about the mess caused by the swallows who nested, year after year, under the eaves.

*   *   *

Both Robin's children were taught that it is unforgivable to kill something merely because you are afraid of it. Both remembered all their lives the closing lines of the poem their father used to quote about the man who threw a log at the snake that came to drink at his water-trough, then regretted it:

> And so I missed my chance with one of the lords
> Of life.
> And I have something to expiate;
> A pettiness.

On the rare occasions that they had met, Anthony and Annie had argued ferociously and got on rather well: this had been a small but important source of happiness to Robert. (A small but important source of discomfort during the years of his marriage had been the feeling that Anthony was dropping him.) And it was Anthony who on Easter Saturday, when they met again, came up with the obvious solution and said, 'But Robert, why does it have to be Easter or nothing? Why can't she come at the beginning of May for heaven's sake?'

'Chloe's invitation was for Easter.'

'I must say, I would have *thought* that if Chloe doesn't mind you – all right, I won't say it, let's call it being madly uxorious – anyway, I would have thought that if she doesn't mind it at Easter then she'd quite likely be able to tolerate the idea with similar equanimity on May Day.'

This conversation had arisen when Anthony – himself in a happy mood – had explained, 'Ah well, I suppose spring is always the season when a young man's fancy turns to thoughts of love, isn't it?' adding, 'Though if I may say so you seem to be looking remarkably hangdog and tail-between-the-legs, as it were, Robert,' and then, after an assessing look, 'After all, on a good day and in a good light you could pass as *relatively* youthful, you know.' (Anthony was six months younger.)

The conversation ended when Robert looked at his watch and realised that he'd have to leave if he was to keep his promise and get back in time to take Chloe to the late-night service to celebrate the Resurrection of Christ.

'Happy Easter, Anthony,' he said.

'You too, Robbie. And Happy Birthday. Just ask Chloe. She'd bite your balls off if you gave her half a chance but I dare say she won't eat you.' And Anthony kissed him ceremoniously three times on the cheek: left, right and then left again.

'The female of the species is deadlier than the male,' Chloe had written. 'A male point of view, no doubt, probably simply reflecting the fact that in some species the female eats the male after mating. Logically speaking, you could see this merely as a very economical use of valuable protein. From the female point of view you would of course have to substitute another word for "deadlier", "stronger" perhaps or "more enduring". The endless cycle of death and resurrection is reserved for young male gods.'

They arrived home not long after midnight, Chloe having said, 'I don't want to stay for the rest of the service, it goes on for hours.' The previous evening they had entered the church in the wake of the returning procession; Chloe had given Robert a little push, indicating that he should move to the right side of the church where the men stood and leave her among the women. The chanting was incomprehensible to him, the atmosphere heavy with incense, the heat given off by all the candles intense, so that he had been glad of their rather slow walk home in the cool, fresh air.

For the Resurrection service, however, he had said with

a firmness that surprised both of them, 'We're going by car tonight.' The frenzy of firecrackers and gunshots that greeted the Resurrection of Christ made him doubly glad to settle Chloe into the front seat of the car, though his reason for wanting to drive in the first place had been a sense that she'd found the previous evening's walk more effort than she would admit. He smiled privately in the darkness as he recalled Anthony's verdict on firearms and virility but merely remarked that someone in the village seemed to have a machine gun.

'No,' she said (listening), 'it's an automatic repeating rifle.'

The fact that Chloe took his lighted candle from him and carried both his and hers carefully back home in the car surprised Robert, but he made no comment.

Except the Lord build the house, they labour in vain that build it; except the Lord keep the city, the watchman waketh but in vain.

When they got back, 'Wait,' she said as he made to open the door, and held their candles under the lintel until with the soot of their smoke she had traced the sign of the cross. (He had indeed noticed the other, more faded crosses over the door but had not associated them with Chloe.) 'It's magic of a sort,' was the only explanation she gave. 'I am supposed to say to you "Christ is risen" but I'd prefer to say "Happy Birthday". Please bend down.' She kissed him on both cheeks, right then left.

It was not until he had gone upstairs and had a pee and cleaned his teeth and undressed and got into bed and turned off the light that it suddenly occurred to Robert to wonder how she knew it was his birthday.

14

At the breakfast table Chloe said, 'There is something that I would like you to have, Robert, and it is this. I have been thinking for some time that you would appreciate it and your birthday seems as good a day as any for me to give it to you.' What she was putting into his hands was her book of Greek myths.

Robert could not help saying, 'Goodness, Chloe, are you sure . . .'

'Of course I'm sure' (a trifle tartly). 'I never do anything without being sure. It would be more gracious if you simply said "thank you".'

'I do thank you. I didn't mean to be ungracious, I do thank you very much, I shall treasure it.'

'Good,' she replied.

Robert, who had been eating bread and honey, said, 'I think it's a book that requires clean fingers, wait a minute,' and went and washed his hands.

Chloe watched him as he turned the pages carefully; he was looking at the illustrations slowly, one by one, without comment. Each illustration was mounted on thick, dark-brown paper and protected by a leaf of tissue paper. He paused at the picture of the cypress trees and the dwelling of Eros, turned a couple of pages, paused again at Psyche, lamp in hand as she bent over sleeping Eros with his fair curly hair and his youthful naked body decently veiled by a fine sheet, paused even longer at Medea who stood before a dark pool in a forest clearing, her long black hair loose, her arms bare, her pleated, ankle-length garment a deep Prussian blue.

'They're exquisite, and what's more they have an intense *presence*,' was all he said.

Medea was a witch, Chloe thought, who was probably capable of tenderness until it all went wrong. What she said was, 'Yes. I have had this book for seventy-five years, Robert. I hope that one day you will pass it on to someone else.'

At which point Robert amazed himself by looking up and saying, 'I wish I had a child.'

Chloe said nothing.

Tenderness is what makes the difference. Tenderness is what other people cannot see; tenderness, even more than desire, is what cannot be thwarted.

In the hottest hour of noon a slight breeze arises as cooler air moves from the sea over the land. They are several miles inland, but nevertheless a faint whispering susurration stirs the reeds and plays on damp, sweaty bodies. They are quiet and still: he is lying on his back and caressing her hair as she lies between his legs with her head resting on his belly. She moves slightly and with extreme gentleness takes his testicles in her mouth. In the whole of the rest of his life no one else ever does this, nor has she ever done it to anyone else.

Tenderness is painful to remember.

Jeremy and his landlady both felt a certain reticence and thus had spent several half-hours in what he thought of as her parlour circling conversationally around the subject that interested both of them. The overt excuses for these sessions were the small cups of thick, sweet coffee that she served and the spoonfuls of even sweeter preserved fruit presented with a glass of water. Jeremy thought of these latter as 'spoons of jam' and disliked them (his mother, who had a slightly phobic difficulty in swallowing pills, had always when her children were young given them whatever pills they needed crushed up in a teaspoonful of jam, and the combination of sweetness and bitterness, syrupiness and grittiness, had put Jeremy off jam for life). However, not wishing to give offence and feeling that it was all in a good cause, he managed to get these cloying spoonfuls down as best he could with the help of the glass of water.

What the landlady succeeded in eliciting was that Jeremy was indeed the son of the snake-lover but that either he knew nothing about anything or else he was too pathologically discreet – unlikely at his age – to be forthcoming. She thus became vaguer herself.

What Jeremy thought he had established was as follows. First, that Chloe's husband had been a difficult man – 'very proud'. Second, that Chloe never visited his grave, that this produced an extremely unfavourable impression, and that paying a couple of workmen once a year to clean the gravestone and cut back the dry grass was not the same thing at all. Third, that one couldn't really blame her, that she'd had trials and tribulations enough and to spare. Just because she was a heretic didn't mean she was a witch, only ignorant people would believe such a thing. Fourth, that doctors didn't really know what they were doing and that it was a great disgrace to play God and to keep people alive who'd be better off dead. (At this point there was a long digression about friends and neighbours who'd suffered at the hands of the medical profession or been kept alive artificially simply so that their families would have to pay bigger bills, followed by certain lurid details of her own medical history which rather embarrassed Jeremy since he wasn't used to discussing such matters.) And fifth, that these things happen, ah well, that mixed marriages aren't really a good idea, that everyone knows there's always trouble if the husband is too old for his wife and that anyway, even if she was to blame, no doubt she'd paid for it.

None of this helped very much.

Jealousy, thought Chloe, is perhaps not only a question of possessiveness. Perhaps the breeding ground for jealousy is the inability to understand the frame within which the other person's feelings are formed.

A few nights later she wrote: 'It is possible that the marriage of Medea and Jason was doomed from the start simply because she was a foreigner and they did not understand one another. The same could be said to be true for Othello and Desdemona.'

This was a rather hesitant train of thought; she paused for a long time, reflecting, then gave up and put down her pen.

The following evening she turned over the page firmly and returned to thoughts of the garden, to the consummate economy of bulbs in which the whole of the future year's growth lies ready stored, to the simplicity of this device by which plants may flourish in winter and spring, then withdraw their energy and retire to lie dormant through the long, hot, dry summer. 'Reptiles hibernate, bulbous plants aestivate,' she wrote, not remembering that in the hottest parts of the world some reptiles may aestivate as well.

'I like simplicity,' she told Robert as they walked round the garden.

'Annie, it's very simple, just say you can come,' he told her when he telephoned on Easter Day.

'I'd love to,' she said, so that in fact it was perfectly simple.

*   *   *

161

'Itchy, witchy, let's get bitchy,' said Anthony. (This prelude to a good gossip had been borrowed from a slightly older friend who remembered the early children's television programmes of the fifties: Anthony, although not aware of its origins, liked the phrase.) He proceeded to tell Robert some rather startling news about a common acquaintance, then surprised him by adding judiciously, 'Actually, I very much doubt that it's true, even if it does make a good story.'

'I'm quite sure it cannot possibly be true.'

'Oh' (lightly) 'I wouldn't ever be too sure about anything, people can do the oddest things . . . I dare say even you, if you ever . . . mmm, shall we say *unbuttoned* slightly, might one day find yourself indulging in the occasional spot of unconventionality.' (Anthony had been going to say 'if you ever let your hair down' but it occurred to him just in time that Robert might be a tiny bit sensitive about not having quite so much hair these days.)

What Robin likes is first to take off Chloe's clothes and then, when she stands before him naked, to remove the hairpins slowly, one by one, and let her long dark hair fall free over her thin shoulders. What Robin likes is for Chloe to sit on top of him, leaning forward until her hair falls like a magic curtain enclosing their faces. Sometimes both cry out aloud as he grasps these dark locks and pulls her down on him hard. 'My witch,' he says, 'don't ever cut your hair off, promise me that.'

'Can I ask you something, Robert?'

Jeremy sounded unusually hesitant, so that Robert wondered what was coming next, hoping that he'd prove adequate if advice or guidance of the older brother or *in loco parentis* variety turned out to be needed. They were driving back to town on the afternoon of Easter Sunday; the roads being deserted, Robert had been rather enjoying driving fast on the straight bits.

'Yes, of course.' (He slowed down.)

'Do you know if Chloe ever had any children?'

This at any rate wasn't too difficult. 'Not as far as I know – she doesn't seem to have children and certainly she's never said anything to suggest that she ever did have a child, but of course if she'd had one and it died I wouldn't know.' As an afterthought, 'Why?'

'I just wondered.'

They drove on in silence for the next kilometre or so.

'Does she speak much of the past?'

'No.'

Jeremy felt that some explanation was needed and said rather disingenuously, 'I was simply thinking that someone her age must have an awful lot of memories.' This sounded feeble, even to himself, but Robert made no comment.

Chloe, worrying like a small and obstinate terrier at the whole idea of truth and memory, sometimes felt that it might be comforting if one could let go of it and convince oneself that one had quite simply made everything up. 'The trouble is,' she said to herself, 'that although I can no longer *see* anything, it is all there like an elusive mote in the periphery of my vision, like a persistent faint ringing in my ears.' The only thing that came back to her at night undimmed – sweet and sharp and disturbing – was his smell.

Different parts of the brain are responsible for the sense of smell and for the other senses. The front part of the brain, she had learned, is responsible for mood, for emotion. The left hemisphere controls speech. It is, of course, extremely complicated, as someone had once told her. 'We are talking in very simplified terms,' he said (and drew a schematic diagram for her).

*   *   *

It was not until his wife was pregnant with Lacerta that Robin, hitherto inexperienced, had been distressed by the dawning of the new idea that Chloe might have been with child when he left her, and doubly distressed by the idea that she had not seen fit to tell him.

In the end, after that miserable train journey, after the night when he sat up late and wrote about loss and other things that could not be spoken of (while Lacerta cried with a thin, high mewing and his wife nursed her), after what seemed like agonising weeks of increasingly clumsy probing of their common acquaintance, he gathered that there was apparently no sign of any child, that Michalis had suffered from something politely referred to as a stroke, that they were now living very quietly and received no visitors.

'Yes,' he had said, 'I quite understand, how terrible for them.' For her. (Robin had in fact been present when this brain damage occurred.)

He thought of writing to her but didn't; the longer he left it, the more impossible it became. In the end, without any accompanying note, he sent her the reptile book and in it those faded petals. The detritus that one can never quite bear to throw away: this was perhaps the message.

I opened to my beloved; but my beloved had withdrawn himself, and was gone: my soul failed when he spake: I sought him, but I could not find him; I called him but he gave me no answer. This passage, however, she only discovered much, much later.

Jeremy, who of course had no means of knowing anything save what he had read, had been preparing himself to meet a putative half-brother or sister and was unable to make up his mind whether he was relieved or sad that no such person appeared to exist. At the very beginning he had in fact wondered for a short time whether Robert might be this person, since he didn't look much like the gardener he claimed to be and his age seemed about right.

At dinner, speaking of the illustrator of the book of myths, Robert said, 'I've never heard of him – though that's probably just my own ignorance. He has quite a lot in common with Dulac but there's a sort of extra dimension of intensity. When I go back, I'll try to find out more about him.'

Chloe said, 'I don't know who he was, but I feel sure he must have spent some time in this country.'

(Both of them, without thinking why, were certain that the illustrator was a man, although no Christian name was given to make this clear, only two genderless initials: E. M.)

Chloe continued rather slowly, formulating the thought as she spoke, 'You see, everyone always talks about the clarity of the light here – it's one of those accepted clichés, isn't it – but actually it would probably be more accurate to talk of the *mercilessness* of the light that strips away all camouflage, all the frills and fuss, and reduces everything to the barest essentials.'

Robert said nothing, waiting for more.

She was suddenly overcome by the need to tell him something: 'Truth and silence,' she said. 'And passion. And they are all quite merciless.'

For some reason Robert felt that this had been a private conversation, which was perhaps why he did not in the end write to Annie that night as he had been intending to do ('If I post it express tomorrow she'll get it before she leaves'), but instead lay in bed and read Chloe's book slowly and carefully, from cover to cover. An odd sense of familiarity, of something half-remembered, far beyond the simple factual memories of versions of these stories read as a child or encountered in the classroom: I suppose, he thought as he turned off the lamp, it's because these myths are so much part of our cultural heritage that one has just absorbed them. He thought of iconographic conventions, of many trips to the National Gallery in his youth. Perhaps they've sort of permeated our consciousness. (Chloe would have told him, 'It's because they are *true*.')

He found the picture of Medea quite extraordinarily erotic, which gave rise to some strange – though not unpleasant – dreams.

Robert worked hard in the garden in the next few days, weeding and raking energetically, mulching with heavy barrow-loads of rich dark compost, repotting all the plants on the terrace. Some of this had to do with an obscure desire to impress Annie with achievement. He also felt a curious need to tire himself physically; thus in the afternoon he more than once set off on long solitary walks over the hills where he found (in random order) a viper sunning itself on a rock, a dead sheep on which hooded crows were feasting, a couple making love, and a rich variety of orchids which he thought Annie would like.

One evening Chloe said dispassionately, 'I imagine that you will naturally want to sleep with her.' And added with a slight smile, 'It is after all hardly dignified at your age to be tiptoeing along corridors trying not to make the floorboards creak.'

He answered, not quite comfortably, 'You very naturally imagine right.'

'Good,' she said. 'It is just that I am thinking logistically, you see, in terms of beds and mattresses.'

Jeremy, whose three months were up, was preparing to return home.

'He is young and strong,' said Chloe, 'he can help you move

the furniture when he comes to say goodbye on Sunday.'

'Fine,' said Robert who felt that he could manage by himself.

'I do not really know,' she mused, 'whether he found what he was looking for.'

This, however, was a silent musing.

He was, presumably, seeking to learn the truth.

For, It is possible, she thought at dinner, that indeed the only thing people are ever in search of is the truth. But Robin's boy is too young to have realised that the more you look for anything, the less you are likely to find it.

Robert noted that she was picking at her food. She was frowning slightly.

'Occasionally,' she said out loud, 'when people come to this country what they lay bare to the pitiless light is some inner part of themselves. I do not think anyone consciously wants or seeks to do this – it is simply something that happens.' A pause. Then, rather quietly, 'I have sometimes wondered whether this is what happened to the nameless man who illustrated the myths and whether this is why his pictures possess so much of what you called intensity and I call silence.' She poured herself a glass of wine and gave him a rather more than usually tentative smile. 'Oh dear, Robert, you will probably think that I have lived alone for far too long and am quite, quite mad.'

'No,' he said, 'no, Chloe, I don't think that.'

It is better to face the truth – provided always that you know it. 'When I go back' he said: these are four little everyday words that express a direct and sure intention set for some finite moment of time, they are anchored, unambiguous words.

Just before dawn Chloe went up the stairs soundlessly on her small bare feet. She held on to the banister for support: I must be tired, she thought. There was no moon and Robert was thus nothing more than a dark shape in the darkness, a faint animal sound of breathing. Sometimes, though, it is hard to distinguish the other person's breathing from your own. Sometimes when you are alone the darkness itself breathes.

The truth is that when he goes back I shall miss him.

15

'The mice have got into it, I'm afraid.' This Chloe pronounced after reviewing with Maria the mattress that she had intended moving into Robert's room; 'We'll have to borrow one,' she declared. Robert was thus detailed to open the gate to a pick-up truck containing three young men and a large, apparently brand-new matrimonial mattress, and then to supervise as this mattress was manoeuvred up two flights of stairs and laid on the old iron-framed double bed that he had already set up in his room. Mattresses being awkward, uncooperative objects to move around, the whole business was slow and inevitably involved a certain amount of comment and conversation of the kind that Robert felt he would rather not have understood; doubtless many nuances escaped him but a wink of cheerful and lubricious complicity from one of the young men (Maria's great-nephew, it seemed) was unmistakable and made him think that Jeremy's assistance would have been preferable. All in all, the preparations for Annie's arrival seemed horribly public. Nothing in a village goes unobserved or uncommented on.

The sheets are of fine-grained linen, carefully ironed (for linen is even cooler than cotton on hot summer nights). She goes upstairs to his room at dusk the evening before he is due to arrive. Her excuse, should anyone observe or comment, is the vase of flowers she is carrying: branches of pale-blue plumbago and stiff, greenish half-opened spikes of acanthus flowers. She closes the door and lies face down on his bed, imagining a warmth in the cool sheets, a dampness, a stray pubic hair perhaps, the impress of his shape, imagining the scent of a hot and tired male body. She lies there until darkness falls. An owl hoots, the smell of freshly watered earth rises from the garden. When she gets up the sheets are very slightly rumpled though still pristine; the flowers she has brought are scentless and the room is redolent of polish and of freshly laundered linen.

When Robin goes to bed the following night he thinks he is imagining the faint trace of her scent on the pillow.

Jeremy's last Sunday lunch began awkwardly. With each of the three of them preoccupied with private anxieties, the conversation flagged. Chloe had instructed Maria to lay the table on the terrace, then fretted that there was too much sun. Jeremy politely offered to change places with her so that she would not have the sun in her eyes; 'I enjoy the sun,' he said, lying valiantly (in fact his fair skin burned easily), then, in a last clumsy effort to draw her, 'I always used to hope that we'd come to Greece for our summer holiday, but for some reason my father never wanted to.'

'Yes,' she replied in tones of chilly disdain, 'tourists and people who know no better invariably think they like the sun.' She regretted the cruelty of this almost immediately, which led her to fuss and to send Robert off to find his gardening hat for Jeremy to wear, after which she retreated into a forbidding silence.

From Easter onwards the influx of holiday-makers begins. Anthony had been moaning that it was almost time to start battening down the hatches: 'It's all very well for you, Robert, safely tucked away as you are in Princess Chloe's enchanted tower, but I have to live in a state of siege all summer. Hordes of hugely obnoxious people everywhere, eating their revolting hamburgers, they drink too much then piss on my doorstep at night, my heartfelt wish is that they all get mad-cow disease *rapidly*.'

Since Anthony lived over a flower shop in a quiet part of town well away from the waterfront and Robert had always associated summer nights in his flat with the scent of gardenias, he took this to be an exaggeration, presumably arising from a distempered mood. However, on the previous Saturday night he had found that in order to ring Anthony's doorbell he was obliged first to squeeze past a rather large motorcycle with foreign number plates and then to disturb a youthful couple – its riders perhaps – who stood closely entwined in the doorway. When he mumbled, 'Excuse me,' they shifted sideways wordlessly, without disentangling from their embrace.

Later the atmosphere eased. In an attempt to recover his poise Jeremy drank slightly more wine than he was accustomed to and as a result got an insistent fit of hiccups, to his great embarrassment.

'Drink water out of a glass backwards,' suggested Chloe, pouring him some, but this remedy failed.

'Annie has an infallible cure,' offered Robert and instructed Jeremy to get up and stand with his back against the wall of the house. 'It's easier to do it if you're lying down,' he explained in all seriousness, 'but if the worst comes to the worst in an emergency you can always do it against a wall. You have to do it so hard that it hurts.'

Jeremy giggled in spite of the hiccups, Chloe rather improbably laughed out loud; Robert swore inwardly and coloured a bit but nevertheless proceeded to press his fist hard into the bottom of Jeremy's ribcage and to hold it there until the hiccups ceased.

Chloe watched the conjunction of their two bodies in the brief intimacy of this cure against the faded, sunlit, apricot-coloured wall. A wash of inchoate tenderness: her irritation evaporated.

A swift and indiscreet encounter behind the outhouses in the early morning cool. 'I'm sorry,' Robin says, 'I hurt you.' 'No,' she answers, 'it's all right, only you should have given me time to get used to the smell of you again first.' A quarter of an hour later he is thanking her politely as she pours his breakfast coffee. Formal conversation about his plans for the summer.

By the time Maria came to clear the dishes all three of them were more relaxed. As she served coffee, Jeremy (regaining confidence) said, 'Chloe, I've got something for you.' He delved into his canvas bag and produced a sheet of paper on to which he'd copied a couple of lines of ancient Greek. 'I came across it by chance without any attribution in a book on typography,' he went on, 'It's a fragment of something which I don't recognise and I'm afraid I haven't managed to track it down yet, but I thought you might like it anyway.'

'Translate it, please,' she asked. (A faint, barely perceptible tightening of lips and heart at the sight of his bag, no longer a shuddering contraction of the entrails.)

'It's called *To a Swallow*,' said Jeremy, and recited: 'And you, dear swallow, arrive each year in summer and weave your nest, while in winter you disappear once more to the Nile or to Memphis, but love is ever weaving its nest in my heart . . .'

'Swallows don't weave their nests, they build them from mud and saliva,' Chloe reflected, not for the first time. Strange: perhaps the poet knew more about love than he did about birds. She smiled at Jeremy. 'Thank you,' she said, folding the sheet of paper. 'I do like it and I shall keep it.'

When he left she took his hand in both of hers and said, 'Come back one day.'

'I'd love to come towards the end of summer with my girlfriend.'

'I don't know if I shall still be here, but come anyway.'

As they drove back to town Jeremy asked, 'Is Chloe planning to go away?'

After a brief pause Robert replied as gently as he could, 'I think she probably meant dying.'

The following day she sat on the bench by the cistern and said to Robert, 'It's not always easy, is it?' Then, realising that her train of thought was obscure, added, 'I mean geographical separations.'

'We can't go on like this,' he says. And, 'I don't think I can come back any more.' (This is the second last summer.) 'Apart from anything else, I've already caught, recorded and illustrated every single reptile on this blasted island, I've even killed and dissected half of them for good measure.' He is vehement. 'Leave him,' he urges, 'leave him, Chloe, and come with me.'

He does not communicate with her all winter. She lives with the emptiness. Yet the following year he returns, albeit later than usual, when the swifts and swallows already have fledglings in their nests.

After Jeremy's departure Chloe went down to the library late at night and selected a volume of the Greek lyric poets; she then sat at the kitchen table, opened a new exercise book and copied out the poem from the *Anacreontea* – once familiar – of which Jeremy had given her the first lines (it occurred to her that had Jeremy known how the poem continued he might not have offered it to her):

'. . . love is ever weaving its nest in my heart. One desire has wings, another is still an egg, yet another half-hatched already: the gaping-beaked fledglings are constantly clamouring; little loves are fed by bigger ones and then, when fully grown, beget others in their turn. What remedy can there be? I have no strength to shout down all these loves.'

This, I suppose, is a more sensible way to live, she thought. Perhaps he lived like this – I have never had any idea. She slipped Jeremy's paper between the pages of her exercise book and wrote his name for the first time: 'Robin was my summer lover, my sweet, sleek bird of passage.' A pause, then, as a new feeling which had been slowly swelling within her emerged into words, 'I am glad at least that Robin had a son.' (For some reason the existence of Robin's daughter was not very real to her.)

There are some words which are spiky and hard to write, while others flow easily from the pen, round and mellifluous; 'Robin' is an easy word to write.

I hope that he was happy.

'To say that she separated from her husband is rather misstating the case,' declared Anthony. 'What she actually did was take him to Athens and dump him in a padded cell. She only brought him back to bury him – and then, by all accounts, danced naked on his grave at midnight.'

'You made that up,' said Robert.

'Yes,' said Anthony, 'quite right, that last bit was an embellishment of my own devising.' He added, 'The rest is true enough though.'

'I don't think,' said Robert slowly, 'that you should blame her.'

Chloe, browsing in the *Anacreontea*, found another poem whose opening lines arrested her: 'It is hard not to fall in love, it is hard to fall in love, but hardest of all is to fail in love.'

Doors that open or close. A small figure sitting straight-backed and very still in the quiet kitchen.

'Boundaries and crossroads and entrances,' she said, 'are the places where dangers lie. Once upon a time people used penises to keep them safe.'

It was May Day and Robert was helping her hang a wreath on the front door. This statement seemed odd, even by Chloe's standards; he wondered whether she had meant to say it, began to murmur some reassuring noncommittal assent, then changed his mind. 'I'm sorry,' he heard himself say firmly, 'but I haven't got a clue what you're talking about.'

'Ah,' she made a little moue of approval as she viewed the wreath in position. 'Yes. Herms,' she explained. 'Schematic statues of Hermes, pillars with a bearded male head and an erect phallus. In antiquity they were held to have powerful apotropaic properties and were placed at boundaries and crossroads and doors to avert evil. The threshold,' she went on, 'the entrance, is the place that above all requires protection. This is why even today no one sees any incongruity in calling upon disparate deities to keep it safe, and this, you see, is why I have both a cross from my Easter candle on the lintel and a May wreath of flowers on the door itself.'

Robert, who had been making several drawings of doorways recently, was interested. 'What about the garlic?' he asked. (The previous summer he had noted that across the threshold of each of the doors that led from house to garden lay a little trail of garlic cloves; in the last few days they had appeared once more.)

'Oh,' she laughed, 'that isn't magic, Maria puts it there when the weather gets warmer, garlic is supposed to keep scorpions out of the house – though I've no idea whether this is merely an old wives' tale or whether it really works.' She added smiling, 'Anyway, at least it means you don't have to be worried about vampires, Robert.'

'I never was,' he said, and the conversation ended.

At lunch, however, she reverted to the subject briefly. 'It's not that I literally *believe* in these things,' she explained, 'just that somehow it seems fitting to follow the old traditions.'

'You like rituals,' he said with a smile.

'Yes. Exactly.'

'I worship your cock,' she tells him one day in the quivering silence of the midday heat. 'Well,' he replies, lazy and detumescent, 'then you are following a very ancient tradition indeed.' 'Is that your classical education speaking?' (She can't resist teasing.) 'Good Lord, no,' he says, 'just common sense.'

With my body I thee worship, Chloe was to read many years later, and wondered who had worshipped whom, how over the passage of those distant summers this balance had subtly come to change. He was growing up, she thought.

Robert made a pen-and-ink drawing of a secret doorway, its door invitingly ajar, flanked by a powerful protective herm. He thought of giving it to Chloe but in the end didn't. To Annie, when he showed it to her the following week, he explained, 'I suppose it felt somehow personal and I was a bit shy about it.'

Annie's perceptions had perhaps been honed by his absence; she told him quite cheerfully, 'I like your series of mysterious doors, Robert,' and thought to herself, not quite so cheerfully. 'His drawings are all about transition and change.'

For there is no doubt that separations and renewals are not

always easy to manage. Some of the faint awkwardness of the first few hours after Annie's arrival was probably due to the fact that neither of them was able to switch instantly into a state of openness. When they met at the airport Annie put down her suitcase and hugged him quite unselfconsciously; Robert was obscurely disappointed by the nature of this embrace, felt that it was the way she would have greeted her brother, yet found himself unable to do anything but respond in kind. In the car he might have kissed her properly on the lips; however, having failed to find a space in the rather limited car park he had left the car beneath a 'No Parking' sign, with the result that he had to drive off rapidly to the accompaniment of a policeman's shrill and determined whistle.

Annie in turn felt that Robert was somehow withdrawn or witholding himself. She was secretly impressed by his lawless parking but couldn't say so. She heard herself talking too much – news of home, news of Hetty – and wished he would say something effective.

A slightly strained wariness.

The only good thing, as Robert realised, was that at the airport his symptoms had magically disappeared. For he had paid several visits to the lavatory that morning, convinced that he'd eaten something that disagreed with him and miserably aware that this was an inauspicious condition in which to welcome Annie. (When he told her about it quite a lot later that night she said, 'Never mind, love, it wouldn't have mattered in the least,' and felt amused affection rather than the customary tinge of irritation with which she usually reacted to the various occasional manifestations of what she had always privately called 'Robert's nerves'.)

Chloe, at dinner that first evening, was gracious and a trifle distant and sat extremely straight-backed in her chair with her ankles neatly crossed and her thin wrists resting lightly on the table. The meal was rather more elaborate than usual and was served by Maria.

Who, during a kichen consultation about food the following morning, scolded: 'You ought to make more of an effort to be pleasant to her.'

'You are being impertinent,' snapped Chloe.

Maria, undaunted, finished what she wanted to say. 'Every man needs a wife and you should be glad he's got one.'

In spite of the presumed epic encounter with the Dutch tourists and in spite of that meeting in the narrow alley by the market, the truth is that Maria had sometimes wondered a little about Robert's friendship with Anthony; regarding these matters, however, she had kept her own counsel. The advent of Annie seemed to put everything into a much more appropriate context. She had thus made up the bed with Chloe's best linen sheets, carefully washed and ironed, and a bridally white crocheted cotton cover, retrieved from the depths of a chest and also freshly laundered. (Annie, who loathed ironing, had fingered the sheets and said, 'God, the labour involved . . .')

Chloe thought of saying, 'They are not married,' but preferred to drop the subject.

As she wandered in the garden in the morning sunlight she saw a hoopoe, but kept this pleasure to herself and did not mention it to Robert.

'Robert told me what a wonderful garden it was,' said Annie, 'but even his descriptions didn't do it justice.' She went on, 'I suppose the one thing you can never fake in a garden is age. Even if you buy ready-made, I mean ready-grown, trees at great cost, nothing ever has that sort of expansive, settled look that comes with time. Walls and paths and everything else always shout "newness" at you.'

'That is so,' assented Chloe. 'This garden was already old when I was born.'

'I love the way you have kept it – somehow wild and immaculate at the same time.'

A fractional unbending: 'Robert has helped me,' Chloe said.

She watched a magpie perch and sway rather improbably on the topmost tip of the tallest cypress tree, then lowered her binoculars and watched Annie kiss Robert: not a passionate embrace but a small, intimate, momentary contact of flesh.

Magpies are large, aggressive, predatory creatures who wreak great havoc on the nests of more delicate birds. I would not have minded so very much if he'd shot magpies, Chloe thought – though in those days, as she recollected, there seemed to have been fewer of them around. She raised the binoculars once more. The magpie had flown off. She sat for a while and studied the close dark foliage of the cypress tree moving slightly in the breeze, the old, enduring, furrowed wood of its trunk.

You cannot fake your age. She is probably a couple of years older than Robert, thought Chloe coolly (correctly, as it happened). She is a large black-and-white sort of person.

Chloe's binoculars were a precision instrument made in Jena about sixty years earlier. They were kept in a battered leather case on the table in front of her bedroom window; once they had been kept on a shelf in the library – but that was when Michalis used them. Where their original owner had kept them she had no idea.

In one of the lonelier moments she had once thought that large trees wait and watch. The observed becoming the observer.

Shortly before Annie arrived Robert thought he had woken one night and become aware of Chloe's presence: a small shape vaguely distinguished against the faint difference in darkness that must be an open door. He had lain quite still and quiet, as in a dream where for some reason one can neither move nor speak. The following morning at breakfast Chloe smiled and greeted him in her normal brisk manner, so that in the end Robert decided that it must indeed have been a dream – a tranquil experience, not an unpleasant one. Being much given to trying to understand his dreams, he puzzled on and off for a couple of hours as to what it might mean, then gave up. After their conversation about herms he wondered briefly if it was the open door that was the significant point.

He told nothing of this to Annie. All the same, when she arrived he found himself rather wishing at first that there had been a key to the bedroom door. After a slight initial hesitation, however, it did not seem to matter.

16

'I've always rather liked minding other people's business,' said Anthony. 'To be really honest, there *are* times when other people's lives do seem to be a tiny bit more exciting than the dreary wasteland of one's own existence.'

This was said apropos of various reminiscences as they drove along dark and winding country roads on their way to a taverna that Anthony liked. Later, as they waited for the owner to come and tell them what he could offer that evening ('No point whatsoever consulting the menu in a place like this,' declared Anthony, 'their menus seem to bear at best a tenuous relation to reality'), Annie shivered under the lush foliage of the mulberry trees and Robert set off back to the car to fetch her jacket.

In one of those sudden leaps of confidence (sometimes regretted later) she said, 'Actually, my life would be a bit of a wasteland if Robert didn't come back.'

'He's the faithful type,' said Anthony comfortably, 'of course he'll come back.' A pause. Then, 'You may simply have to be a teeny bit patient, that's all, I'd allow him a minuscule amount of leeway if I were you, Annie darling, and not boss him around more than you can help.'

What Annie really wanted to ask Anthony, but of course couldn't, was, 'Is there someone else?'

'Make allowances for her,' Robert said, 'she's old and set in her ways and has lived alone for so long that she's got out of the habit of having guests. Don't take it to heart if she's a bit brusque.'

She never asks him if he has someone else. She assumes he does. She has always known that one day he will not come back.

'You will have just to take each day as it comes,' they said, at which she wondered: What on earth else does anyone ever do? Someone also said, 'He's extremely lucky to be alive.' They meant no harm, on the contrary they were well-meaning men, serious and overworked and no doubt kindly. 'And yet,' she thought, 'their crassness beggars belief.'

She later reflected that 'I didn't mean any harm' could never serve as an excuse for anything: it is merely the child's wail over something irretrievably broken.

To Jeremy, lover of Sophocles, she had said, 'The most tragic passage in *Oedipus* is the speech of the shepherd who confesses to having saved the baby exposed to die. Out of his simple, pure, human act arose all the agony that followed.'

You cannot, she thought, mistake rightness and simplicity and purity, and there is little point attempting to apologise for the pain that comes in their wake. Good intentions count for nothing, they are ultimately irrelevant: this is a bleak view of life.

Yet it is of course equally true that this pain cannot be mistaken, or the anguish or the guilt, in spite of the complicated way in which these feelings get in the way of each other. Unable to explain to the only man who bothered to ask that guilt seemed merely an irritating distraction from pain, Chloe had retreated into icy hauteur; 'A whining mosquito, a bothersome fly to be swatted,' was what she might have said about such guilt, but found it easiest to tell him to mind his own business.

'You ought to be ashamed of yourself,' someone else had said and had spat at her (this was a woman in the village and it was after this episode that Chloe locked the gate).

Sufficient unto the day is the evil thereof she read one night when Robert and Annie had gone to have dinner with their friend, and doubted whether this was true, although, 'The more I think about it, the less I understand what this phrase might mean,' she mused. An abiding regret for words that should not have been spoken: even in such circumstances a wife should find kinder words for her husband.

One of the things that Robert had always admired in Annie was her capacity for allaying worry. A solidity, an immutability, a boundless certainty. 'Never mind, love,' were comforting words that had once soothed Hetty's minor childhood mishaps and were now applied equally kindly to Robert's major adult failure in timing; 'I dare say we're both out of practice,' she added. (This was reassuring to him on more than one level, with the result that it did not occur to him that she might be very tentatively fishing.)

Indeed, the reason why Annie would have liked in turn to seek reassurance from Anthony was quite simply the fact that, after what she chose to call 'the initial hiccups' had been sorted out, Robert's love-making seemed rather more masterful than the way she remembered it. Someone taught him this, was the half-thought in her mind, but it seemed impossible to ask.

If she asks Robin nothing it is perhaps from a sense that the hours they spend together belong to another dimension: a silent world outside time and place. Within this silence, to the accompaniment of cicadas, minds and bodies meet, and indeed they speak and laugh and teach each other things.

'Wait,' she says, and, 'I can't,' he says. Then, 'Sorry.'
Then, a little later, 'Perhaps I ought to call you "Hedyla".'
'Why?' 'Because Martial had a boyfriend called Hedylus and
sometimes they didn't get their timing quite right – he wrote an
epigram about it. Though in fact in their case it was Hedylus
who was too hasty.'

Just before dinner he finds her alone on the terrace and gives
her a sheet of paper; 'I made a translation of it for you,' he
says. She reads:

Cum dicis 'Propero, fac si facis,' Hedyle, languet
protinus et cessat debilitata Venus.
Expectare iube: velocius ibo retentus.
Hedyle, si properas, dic mihi, ne properem.

'Which is to say' (Robin had written) 'freely rendered,'

When you say, 'I cannot wait, come if you're going to come,'
I slacken at once, I lose it, Hedylus.
Bid me go slow: by trying to hold back, I'll all the faster come.
If you can't wait, Hedylus, just tell me 'wait'.

Chloe folds this paper and puts it safely away and smiles at
him over the dinner table.

On another occasion he explains, 'What I like about the
Roman poets is that they were never afraid to talk about the
things that go wrong as well as the things that go right.'

His son had declared, 'What I love about it is the subtle,
muscular economy of the language.' And then, 'The most
brilliant, wonderful alliterative line in all Greek poetry is in
Oedipus.'

'Tell me,' she had said, amused by his youthful enthusi-
asm.

And Jeremy had explained, 'It's when Oedipus doesn't want to know what Tiresias knows and accuses him of being blind,' and had pushed the hair back from his forehead and quoted, '*Typhlos ta t'ota ton te noun ta t'ommat'ei*,' adding for Robert's benefit, 'which means "you are blind in your ears and your mind and your eyes" – he really spits it at him.'

A sweeping denial of reality: a desire not to see. In the end what Oedipus did with his guilt was put its eyes out.

'There is blindness and there is seeing,' Chloe now wrote. 'There is watching and being watched.' Not particularly comfortable thoughts. There is sometimes the knowledge of being watched.

'Oh God, we can't,' said Annie, 'not here.'

'There's not a soul for miles around,' said Robert, and then, rather amazingly, 'and even if there were, why should it matter?'

They were high up on a lonely hillside looking at orchids. (Chloe had said, 'Don't pick any orchids, will you, or try to dig them up – their relationship to their environment is complicated and fragile, they don't transplant well.')

Chloe watched Robert closely and admitted to herself rather grudgingly that the slight extra stooping she had noticed on the day of Annie's arrival had disappeared. When you have been observing someone carefully for several months you come to feel a strange kind of intimacy, a familiarity with the small signs of discomfort or of awkward diffidence – or conversely of ease. Chloe made very great efforts.

I don't think I'd much care for the sort of garden she designs, Chloe thought, her gardens would have careful colour combinations and probably things called 'vertical accents', they would not be wild and rampant, but nevertheless she controlled such thoughts (as well as others) and spoke reasonably fluently at the dinner table about plants and plant lore. She tended to retire early. In her nocturnal perambulations she avoided the second floor.

'Will you come out to dinner with us one evening?' asked Robert, 'I'd really like it if you would.'

'Thank you, but do you know I think I won't,' she replied. I do not transplant well.

It was ten minutes or so after this exchange that she spoke of orchids once more, explaining, 'The word "orchis" means testicle in Greek – and if you saw their perfectly formed pair of slightly asymmetrical roots you would understand why the plant bears this name.'

When they were alone Robert told Annie, 'That was a typical Chloe conversation.'

Annie sat at the table in front of the bedroom window picking at a torn fingernail and asked him if he had any nail clippers.

'Yes. In the middle drawer of the table.'

It should be noted that Robert, although apparently tidy and house-trained, allowed himself one small area of untidiness; in spite of much nagging from his former wife and a certain amount of remonstrance on Annie's part as to the need for order if you live in a small space, the inside of what he considered to be his own private drawers remained in a state of disorder. ('I always know where everything is,' he maintained obstinately.) Annie, perhaps remembering Anthony's words, made no comment on the chaos in the drawer, found what she wanted, dealt with her fingernail, then asked, 'Can I look at the rest of your drawings?' (She had spotted the faded cardboard folder in which he kept them.)

'You've seen the ones that matter, but yes, of course, go ahead.'

And thus it was that, tucked away at the back of the folder,

Annie discovered the Valentine's card which Robert had never sent her and which he had somehow put out of mind. This card was drawn with a fine, brown felt-tipped pen on five thicknesses of paper folded and glued to open book-wise, with two of the inner pages cut away so that as each page was turned, more of the drawing that lay behind them came into view. (Robert had once illustrated a book of this kind for very young children.) The first page showed a pastiche Victorian design of hearts and birds and flowers, in the centre of which was the legend *This is a portrait of the man who loves you.* The next page showed the man's head and shoulders and was in fact a fairly successful, if schematic, self-portrait; to one side of his head were the words *He loves you here.* When this page was turned he was revealed to the waist, naked, with a shocking pink heart drawn at chest level and the words *This bit loves you too.* The next page showed him full frontal, both hands arranged in a modest but not quite successful attempt to conceal his erect penis; the caption said *Oh dear, an indiscreet moment, better turn over quickly.* The last page showed him full length, still naked, seen from the back this time, and simply said *No words are enough.*

Annie was so silent that Robert came over to see what she was looking at.

'You never sent it,' she said finally.

'No.' A pause. 'I suppose I thought I might be putting pressure on you or something. Making a fool of myself.'

'How,' she asks, 'can you manage to tell them apart?' She is looking at some of his watercolours of snakes and finds it hard to see much difference between two of them whose colour and markings at first sight appear very similar. He replies, 'Well, obviously you can't always be sure of identifying something correctly, especially when you only get a brief glimpse of it – and to make matters more complicated there's a fair amount

of variation between individuals within the same species – but on the whole when you've got used to looking at them you spot the differences immediately. Look, this one has vertical pupils, for example, whereas the grass snake has round pupils.' 'Is that why you always paint them with their beady eyes wide open?' she asks. 'Yes,' he says, 'indeed it is.' He tries to explain: 'It's like you and plants – you can distinguish at a glance between plants that look much of a muchness to me simply because you are deeply familiar with them.' And then, quietly, 'I wait every day for you to come and join me, I listen for you, I would recognise your footsteps anywhere, Chloe, even in a crowd. It's the same thing.'

I would have recognised your perfectly formed firm young pair of balls anywhere, even in a crowd. Their small asymmetry was always a delight.

There is nothing more fragile than a loved body. What came into Michalis's mind was the idea of spoiling and destroying, not of killing; this is why he armed his rifle and took careful, unhurried aim at Robin's testicles and this is why Chloe spoke cruel words.

'When we get back to work, Robert, I'd like to do something about the irrigation channels.'

Neutral words which Robert, perfectly correctly, interpreted as meaning 'when Annie's week is up and she has gone.' (There were two more days left.) However, The anticipation is always worse than the actuality, he thought to himself rather vaguely, by which he probably meant not so much Annie's imminent departure as the fact that Chloe was behaving herself and Annie seemed happy and unruffled; the idea that these perceptions came to him refracted through the subjective prism of his own contentment did not cross his mind at all. He was unaware of the efforts being made.

He answered, 'OK, fine.'

Annie – who had indeed been feeling rather positive about things for the past couple of days – was for once more sensitive than Robert to the various threads of tension in the atmosphere and thought she had a pretty shrewd idea of their origin.

She asked politely, 'When were they made?'

'I don't know,' said Chloe. 'I imagine about a hundred odd years ago, but they could of course be older. Irrigation channels are like the terracing on the hillsides – well nigh impossible to date. Once people find the best solution to a practical problem, they go on using it for centuries.'

Water was always the *sine qua non* of life without which no garden could be made on this island. 'Try not to waste it,' she had told Robert when he first arrived, and, 'A lot occasionally is better than a little often. Only the pots really need watering every day. Most plants like to drink deep and satiate themselves from time to time rather than be tantalised and frustrated and encouraged into unsustainable growth by an inadequate sprinkling.'

For so many years the only happy smell left in my life was that of hot, dry, thirsty earth gratefully drinking.

As the hart panteth after the water brooks, so panteth my soul after thee, O God. This Chloe reflected on for a while as she explored the Bible. Then, *As in water face answereth to face, so the heart of man to man.* Yes. 'You will see your reflection if you keep still,' he had said. When you are very still you may see your reflection in the other person's eyes.

There is no doubt that a thought held in the mind may

always be subdued and dismissed if need be, while a thought committed to paper is no longer so easy to get rid of – it may take on an insistent, clamouring life of its own. As she sat by lamplight on the terrace, after the table had long since been cleared and Robert and Annie had retired to bed, Chloe did not write directly about why people seek to destroy what is beautiful. All the same, having once written Robin's name she found other things becoming possible; she thus frowned and hesitantly wrote, 'Jealousy is a kind of hate, a gnawing and painful anger that negates all warmth or wit or wisdom. But the truth is that I did not care how he felt.' (Her husband's name apparently did not wish to be written.)

Such thoughts seemed to require a certain physical effort – like pushing open a creaking garden door behind which years and years of fallen leaves and detritus have amassed, like struggling to turn on a tap which has become rusted through disuse. I believe I am rather tired, thought Chloe. She turned off the lamp on the terrace, locked the door and made her way to her room, though she did not sleep immediately.

On Annie's last evening Robert would have very much liked to take her out to dinner – to eat on the waterfront perhaps, and laugh and drink wine or even hold hands surreptitiously under the table (though quite possibly, he thought, Annie would have found this silly and would have taken it as further evidence to support her claim that most men can't seem to get beyond stereotyped sentimentality); however, in the end it seemed more courteous to stay at home and eat with Chloe.

And Chloe in her black silk trousers was in good form, so that the meal passed pleasantly in spite of – or perhaps because of – a power cut which meant that they ate by candlelight: flames dipping and flickering and growing strong once more against the backdrop of the dark garden, shadows against the wall of the house.

'I'm so sorry,' Chloe said, 'it's something that tends to happen from time to time.'

'It's very romantic,' said Annie.

The conversation turned to the use of candles for devotional purposes, with Chloe declaring that it must pre-date Christianity by a long time. 'Candles or little oil lamps,' she said, 'the oil lamps that hang in front of icons are the distant descendants of those that must once have filled the niches cut into the rock around ancient shrines.'

Annie laughed and said, 'Well, they're certainly more magical than the rather nasty little electric candles I saw not long ago in front of the Sacred Heart and Our Lady of the Serpent and so on.'

This interested Chloe. 'What is Our Lady of the Serpent?'

'The Virgin Mary crushing a snake firmly beneath one of her feet, with the infant Jesus in her arms. One of those garish plaster statuettes that you see in suburban Catholic churches.'

'But what does it mean?'

'Your guess is as good as mine,' said Annie cheerfully, 'I know nothing whatsoever about Catholic dogma. I only happen to have seen one recently because I went to a wedding. Maybe something to do with original sin,' she added helpfully.

Chloe lay in bed later and thought, Newer gods are resentful of the abiding power of the older gods that they supplanted: this is why she crushes the serpent.

Robert lay in bed and put his arms round Annie and said, 'Annie, listen, I'm sorry, please bear with me if you can, but I think I'd like to stay with Chloe a little longer.'

Anthony the day before had hugged Annie as they stood together on the pavement while Robert went to get the car and said to her, 'Don't worry.' Then, on Robert's return, had patted him on the shoulder and said, 'Some early nights from now on, Robbie dear. Being in love is utterly exhausting, as we all know. Burning *all* the candles at both their ends.'

At the airport Robert found a space in the car park, took Annie's hand and kissed her tenderly. Just before she went through passport control they embraced once more. 'Take care, Robert,' she said and neither of them found anything remarkable in this slightly uncharacteristic expression. The words that had been on her lips but that she had suddenly for some reason felt it better to censor at the last minute were, 'Be careful, she's in love with you.'

17

Robert watched with fascination as a toad (or maybe a frog: he wasn't sure) shed its skin. It was sitting upright on the damp earth in one of the channels amidst a scatter of fallen mauve petals and was using its front legs to pull the old skin forwards over its head, rather like someone taking off a pullover. It had an air of unhurried concentration and did not seem frightened of him.

This was in the early morning, before the sun had risen high enough to be hot, when the garden still maintained some of the leisurely ease of the night. Chloe had not yet made her appearance; during Annie's stay she had taken to breakfasting alone, in her room presumably, and it seemed that this custom was to continue – at any rate, Maria now set the table on the terrace for one person. These days Robert sometimes did not see Chloe until lunch.

Morning scents of anticipation and freshness. Chloe watched Robert pause, then squat under the jacaranda tree for a few minutes as if absorbed by something, and wondered what he was looking at. I keep watch over him: by watching I make him safe. But this, she told herself severely, is really a very mad thought. She put down her binoculars and thus did not see Robert stand up and raise his eyes briefly to her window.

He made his way to the cold-frame that he had built for cuttings by the compost heap. Three of the pomegranate cuttings which he had made in winter and nursed carefully under a transparent plastic bag on a warm windowsill had rooted; with Chloe's permission, he had given the healthiest-looking one to Annie ('They're yours to do what you like with,' Chloe had said lightly, but Robert could not help feeling that everything in or of the garden was hers and moreover sensed that in spite of her words she was pleased he'd asked.) The fertile scent of rotting vegetation is actually quite pleasant, he thought to himself now. A secretive, female scent, was the unconscious half-thought.

Vigils in hospitals are what is expected of patients' kith and kin. One must simply sit by a white bed and keep watch. One cannot really say, 'I am not doing any good by being here,' far less, 'He would presumably hate me if he regained consciousness and opened his eyes and saw me here beside him.' The only thing she could do was to fan him from time to time, for of course in those days there was no air-conditioning and the September days were hot and humid.

'Look,' she says, 'be reasonable, you will grow out of me one day.' She avoids saying, 'You are young,' yet feels an inward wrench of agony, of tenderness, at the sulky child within him who responds obstinately, 'I am not reasonable and I shall never grow out of you.' The thought that cannot be borne is, One day you might come to hate me: any other pain would be better than this. A short while later she caresses him and tells him, 'Carpe diem,' whereupon he laughs in sudden delight at her use of a phrase he has taught her. And thus the moment passes.

'Yes,' said Chloe, recognising his description at once, 'it was a green toad.'

('It was rather beautiful,' Robert had said, 'creamy white with green markings a bit like irregular-shaped ivy leaves.')

She explained, 'A simple rule of thumb for telling frogs and toads apart is to look at the length of their back legs: imagine the back leg stretched forward alongside the creature's body – if it reaches to about snout level you're looking at a toad, while if it's much longer then what you've got is a frog.' She added, 'I see green toads in the garden from time to time in summer, yet for some reason as far as I know they never breed here like the common toads do. I've always hoped that one year they would. Their call is a wonderful quiet contralto trill.'

'How odd to hear a cricket at midday,' Robin says when he first hears this sound somewhere behind the reeds. The early summer cicadas have fallen silent suddenly in one of those strange orchestrated hushes. She is sitting cross-legged and naked, putting her hair up again; her mouth is full of hairpins and so she does not tell him that it is a toad. Robin in any case has already forgotten it: he is smiling at the beauty of familiar movements, the smooth line from armpit to lifted breast as she raises her arm to the back of her head and disciplines once more her wild, dark witch locks.

They were sitting in the dining-room having lunch. Without thinking about it, Robert no longer found the formality of this room quite so daunting; indeed (for the summer was not yet advanced enough to require closed shutters), the slight signs of shabbiness which the bright sunlight revealed – the faded curtains, the threadbare patch on the rug, the damp stain high up on the wall near the ceiling, the network of cracks in the plaster of the ceiling itself – now gave rise to a sense of comfortable familiarity.

'What really struck me,' he said, 'was the virginal, pristine *newness* of the new skin – smooth and gleaming and brilliantly coloured.'

Chloe smiled. 'Yes,' she said again, 'renewal.' She gave him a brief lesson about the different ways in which different species slough their skin: 'Newts and salamanders wriggle forward out of theirs without using their hands, but lizards, I'm afraid, do it a lot less elegantly, their skin cracks and flakes off bit by bit, so that they go through a dreadful phase of looking psoriatic and scabby.' She said nothing about snakes.

'You're a good teacher, Chloe, I learn all sorts of things from you' (Robert rather liked her in this didactic mood).

She laughed. The conversation meandered gently: lunch had somehow become a relaxed and easy meal.

Robin shows her what he calls the 'spectacles' on a shed snakeskin. 'An excellent adaptation to keep dust out of their eyes,' he says. 'Does that mean that every time they slough their skin they see a brighter and clearer world?' she asks. 'I don't see how one could ever know,' he replies seriously. 'What it does mean is that snakes have no lacrimal ducts or tears.'

At dinner that night she was fairly silent as they began to eat, then said, 'I think one of the reasons that people have worshipped snakes is because of this process of renewal, this periodic re-emergence into a new state of sleekness.'

Robert, who had never worshipped anything, thought of the practicalities: 'It can't be a very comfortable process.'

'No,' she said after a moment's pause, 'I dare say it never is.'

'The thing that one can say for Madame Chloe is that she never seems to have done anything by half-measures. One can't actually help having a certain sneaking admiration.' This was Anthony, in a generous mood; the train of thought had arisen from various pieces of advice he might have given

Robert about Annie, although a sense of delicacy for once prevented him from voicing them. He thus pursued this promising line of gossip: 'As a matter of fact I gather she had a *wildly* passionate liaison with the father of that young man you were so extraordinarily cagey about.'

Robert ignored the last part of this assertion and said quietly, 'I know' (realising that somehow he did know this).

To Annie he wrote at length (though not directly about Chloe). 'Now that you know where I am,' he told her – and she understood what he meant so well that this expression only struck her as amusing when she reread the letter for the third time – 'we can imagine each other much better.' And it is true that in his imagination Robert had finally managed to make the leap from the front door and threshold to the interior of the house, so that he now visualised Annie sitting at the kitchen table going through her accounts, or lying in bed, or brushing her hair in front of the bathroom mirror; indeed it is also true that recently he had been thinking of it as 'our house' rather than 'Annie's house'. 'When I come home we'll see about it,' he wrote more than once in response to various minor domestic worries.

Annie stopped arguing quite so much with Hetty and announced, 'Robert will be coming back when he's good and ready to do so.' She had said the same thing (or words to this effect) more than once before, yet this was the first time that Hetty did not receive a definite impression of whistling in the dark.

'Are you faithful to her?' asked Chloe.

'Almost,' replied Robert, surprised at his honesty yet paying no heed to his rather more surprising lack of resentment at this extremely personal question. 'My wife was unfaithful to me and it hurt like hell,' he added.

'What was it that hurt?' (She seemed interested.)

'Oh, wounded vanity, masculine ego – something like that, I suppose.'

Chloe, who recognised this as an evasive answer, smiled at him encouragingly, so that Robert suddenly found himself telling her about the very worst thing of all, confessed to no one else, the thing that still made him cringe: the fact that when he had surprised his wife and her lover disporting themselves in his bed, what he had done was apologise and close the door discreetly.

'Yes,' she said calmly, 'I can see that that would hurt.'

(When a little while later he had faced his wife in the expectation of some apology perhaps on her part, she had announced rather nastily that his spinelessness was beyond bearing; this, however, Robert did not tell Chloe.)

'To make matters worse, she started divorcing me first.'

'Perhaps she was doing you a favour,' said Chloe, who thought of doors opening and closing.

Perhaps complaisance is what hurts most, perhaps what lay behind his blind desire to destroy were all those unseeing summers of willed ignorance.

The covered cistern was at the highest point in the garden. The irrigation channels – originally connected to the earlier open cistern – had been carefully designed with a system of gates in the form of close-fitting metal sheets that could be raised or lowered to divert water into various parts of the garden. Most of these were now missing, and where they remained were rusted into immobility; 'We'll need new ones,' said Robert. He tried cleaning and oiling the stopcock at the base of the cistern but this too refused to budge.

'Very well,' said Chloe, 'we'll replace it.'

('It's like a complicated railway system with junctions and points,' Annie had said and Robert, who had once played with model railways and had enjoyed the feeling of omnipotence as he switched the points and controlled the trains and averted – or on occasion deliberately caused – derailments, knew just what she meant. Chloe, however, had always seen this age-old irrigation network in more organic terms; 'They are the labyrinthine veins and arteries through which the life-blood circulates,' she told Robert.)

The plumber who replaced the stopcock tried hard to persuade her to install an electric pump but Chloe was obstinate: 'I want to make everything the way it was.'

'No pacemakers?' Robert risked asking.

'Absolutely not.'

The channels had silted up with the passing of the years and Robert had no idea what their depth should be. He paced backwards and forwards trying to calculate gradients, borrowed a spirit-level from someone in the village, started digging.

Having noticed from her window that Robert was bareheaded, Chloe came out to bring him his hat, then seated herself on a nearby bench and watched him work. At the beginning Robert had disliked having to work under observation (a not very comfortable feeling that he was probably doing the task all wrong, that her silence implied criticism, that his body was awkward or his stomach rumbling); however, with time her presence had ceased to be disconcerting and had rather come to seem a companionable habit, so that in fact the mornings when she did not venture out into the garden now felt curiously empty.

He took off his T-shirt quite unselfconsciously. She looked at the muscles in his back glistening with sweat. A faint masculine smell. Neither felt any need to say anything.

'Shut up, Anthony,' said Robert. (This was in response to some delighted variations on the theme: 'It was one of those screwing in public, can't keep out of each other's knickers kind of things.') 'Let it be.'

Anthony, recognising a certain firmness here, changed the subject.

Although he had told Annie of his desire to stay on after the end of the agreed year and had received what he thought of as her permission to do so (in fact a not entirely enthusiastic acquiescence), Robert had not spoken of the subject to Chloe. This was perhaps due to a difficulty in explaining quite why he wanted to remain with her, not very clearly thought out (although woven among the other conscious strands was a reluctance to state too brutally, 'People shouldn't be alone at your age').

Not long after one of these pleasant and amicable mornings in the garden she became once more fidgety and irritable.

'You do seem to be going extraordinarily slowly, Robert,' she declared impatiently as she watched him with the spirit-level.

'Rome wasn't built in a day.'

This attempt at placation did not go down well and Chloe was withering: 'I can't stand people who speak in stupid, meaningless clichés.'

Robert cleared his throat and tried again. 'Chloe, I'm going slowly because I want to get it right,' he said as mildly as possible. 'I want to be sure that the water will flow properly – water won't flow uphill, OK?'

'There is no need whatsoever to be bad-tempered and rude.' And with this chilly retort she got up and left, the dignity of her departure slightly marred by a scattering of sunflower seeds.

Oh dear, thought Robert.

Later in the day though she admitted, 'It is just that I'm anxious to get the work finished before you go,' and he understood that this was by way of apology.

'It will be finished.' A moment's hesitation, then, 'As a matter of fact, I've been meaning to ask you if perhaps I could stay a couple of months longer.'

'Indeed?' (Still bristling.) 'I am actually quite capable of managing by myself.' I have always managed perfectly well alone.

'Yes,' he replied, 'I know that. It's just that I'd like to, it would suit me to stay – if you'll have me, of course.'

'Have you quarrelled with Annie?'

'No.'

A faintly uncomfortable pause.

'I'm sorry,' said Chloe, 'that was really dreadfully impertinent of me, wasn't it?'

Her hand strayed on to the table: a strange and urgent desire to touch him. After a moment Robert gently rested his hand on hers. She resorted to gracious formality and said, 'It would give me great pleasure, Robert, if you were able to stay on for a little while.'

After a certain amount of thought, Jeremy wrote to Chloe. This was in the main a formal, polite letter thanking her for her hospitality; 'I did so much enjoy our Sunday lunches,' he wrote, 'you made me feel very privileged to be allowed to enter such an oasis of beauty and tranquillity.' He enclosed a slim volume. 'I thought that perhaps you might like to have some of my father's translations.'

Chloe did not look at this book immediately but took it upstairs and placed it on the table by her bed beneath – in order of size – the Bible, the Apocrypha and the Book of Common Prayer. That night, in a sudden fit of obsessive orderliness she found herself irked by the fact that the slimmest book of all was at the bottom of the pile and thus placed it on top. The following night she opened it and read the free translation of the epigram to Hedylus (which lay in her cigar box, the sheet of paper beginning to split along the creases where it was folded); this, it seemed, was the only poem addressed to Hedylus – or the only one Robin had seen fit to translate – though young men named Postumus, Diadumenus and Hyllus had two or three each. There was an uncomplimentary piece addressed to a woman called Chloe (one's own name, she thought, always leaps out of the page at one). A lot about licking and sucking partners of one or other sex. A couple of epigrams on the difficulties an older woman faces when trying to find a young man to fuck her. Some of Martial's difficulties with Hyllus seemed to have to do with the fact that the boy was growing up. Chloe turned off the lamp and thought of all these people; the past is by definition dead and gone even if the figures who lived in it remain vivid.

Meister Eckhart wrote, 'The more a thing is in common, the nobler and more valuable it is. I have life in common with those things that live . . .' This had pleased Chloe when she first came across it; it occurred to her now that the words 'the communion of saints' might refer to the *is-ness* of shared experience between all people who have ever lived, indeed, this may even be what 'life everlasting' means. 'My private thoughts are possibly mad and probably blasphemous,' she said to herself, but decided that in neither case did it matter.

'When snakes flicker their forked tongues,' says Robin, 'they are testing their environment, smelling it and tasting it at the same time, checking what is going on around them. Snakes possess something called Jacobson's organs to which their forked tongues transmit scent particles. Lizards also have them.' He adds, 'There are times when I wish I did too.' 'Your forked tongue flickering would feel rather nice,' she agrees. ('Martial was fairly preoccupied with oral sex,' he has just told her.)

But this conversation is an interlude merely, one of those happy moments when more painful things are temporarily forgotten. He is young and miserable: 'If you won't come with me, then I cannot bear staying.' In spite of this he stays. She is older and wiser: more realistic and infinitely more foolish.

Robert said to Anthony, 'I haven't quite finished the work that needs doing in the garden, that's why I'm going to stay on a little while longer.'

Anthony thought of various responses to this but contented himself with saying, 'Fine. Always a delight to have your company, dear child.' (This appellation had infuriated Robert when they were at school but these days no longer bothered him when it occasionally surfaced.) As a parting shot Anthony added, 'Terrible things happened in that garden, or so people declare, I dare say what you're really busy doing is exorcising them. Bell, book and candle.'

'No. Simply spade, hoe and rake.'

Chloe read: *And they heard the voice of the Lord God walking in the garden in the cool of the day: and Adam and his wife hid themselves from the presence of the Lord God amongst the trees of the garden. And the Lord God called unto Adam, and said unto him, Where art thou? And he said, I heard thy voice in the garden, and I was afraid, because I was naked; and I hid myself. And he said, Who told thee that thou wast naked? Hast thou eaten of the tree, whereof I commanded thee that thou shouldest not eat? And the man said, The woman whom thou gavest to be with me, she gave me of the tree and I did eat. And the Lord God said unto the woman, What is this that thou hast done? And the woman said, The serpent beguiled me, and I did eat.*

Another word that begins with 'l' is loss.

18

Late June faded imperceptibly into July. May could at a pinch still be considered spring, and indeed it rained heavily a couple of times after Annie left – relieving Robert of the need to water the garden too often before Chloe's irrigation works were complete. Nevertheless Maria's garlic was already in place and towards the end of the month when Robert went upstairs one day to wash before lunch he found the mosquito net lying over the foot of his bed ready for him to hang from the metal hoop suspended from the ceiling. He smiled to himself as he did so and a couple of days later wrote to Annie, 'I wish we'd had the net when you were here – it's made of some kind of white tulle and gives the bed a thoroughly bridal and private look.' There were times when he felt very alone in this bed.

June, however, is definitely summer, even if there is still a feeling of luxurious expansiveness in the garden; at dawn there is moisture in the atmosphere and at midday the sky is blue, while trees and plants still possess an air of purposeful growth. By July the great heat has set in. Everything is coated in a layer of dust, leaves hang listlessly, at noon the sky is glaringly white. Only at twilight do the cicadas cease their insistent rasping as the garden sighs and rustles and settles itself to breathe more freely during the hours of darkness.

Robert and Chloe sat on the terrace watching the moon rise above the trees.

'I cannot manage to eat two meals a day,' she said, 'please don't press me, I am not ill, I am simply old.' She filled his glass with wine, then half-filled hers and added water. 'To you, Robert,' she said, drinking. 'It is exactly a year since you came here.'

If anniversaries are important, it is because there is a fitting-ness in the cyclical, she thought. There is the perfection of completion: the serpent that devours its own tail.

What this led her to say out loud was, 'Only once in my life have I seen snakes mating.'

He said nothing, waiting for more.

'It is a taboo sight. Tiresias saw it and changed sex as a result. I suppose you could say there's a certain logic in this, if you consider snakes to be chthonic creatures.'

'Making the punishment fit the crime, as it were?'

She laughed. 'Yes, perhaps – especially since what Tiresias did was to throw his staff at them – but what happened next is even more interesting: he chanced upon coupling snakes again and was promptly turned back into a man. When Zeus and Hera asked him the obvious question, which of course he was the only human being in a position to answer – "Which sex has the greater pleasure?" – do you know what he replied, Robert? He said, "Oh women – women every time." I imagine he was right,' she added.

'Well, I have to bow to your superior knowledge there, Chloe.'

'All the same, it was a strange answer for a patriarchal society, wasn't it? And even stranger is the fact that it was Hera, not Zeus, who was so annoyed by it that she struck him blind.'

Something made Robert go back to the beginning of the conversation. 'Were you punished, Chloe?'

She reflected. 'Sometimes I used to think so. But in the end no, probably not, no crime and no punishment.' Another pause, then a laugh. 'Anyway, if there is one thing I cannot stand it is self-pity.'

She attempted that night to write about original sin but gave up, her thoughts too fugitive to find expression in words. Talking to Robert in any case seemed to make writing unnecessary. And indeed this proved to be the last time that she opened any of her exercise books – though for several nights she spent time sorting through them, putting them into chronological order and tying them up in bundles. The last entries were thus a reflection made a week earlier on the god Priapus who rules in gardens and strikes terror into men with his penis (*Tu qui pene viros terres*: 'Possibly women are less frightened,' she wrote), and now a stanza of a poem suddenly dredged up from long, long ago:

> O swallow, sister, O fleeting swallow,
> My heart in me is a molten ember
> and over my head the waves have met.
> But thou wouldst tarry or I would follow,
> Could I forget or thou remember,
> Couldst thou remember and I forget.

(These lines had been nagging at the fringes of her mind ever since the day Jeremy had given her the fragment from the *Anacreontea*; they emerged into memory once more a little while after Robert asked her about punishment.)

Returning late one Saturday night, Robert went up the stairs as quietly as possible in order not to disturb her. Old houses are not silent places though, there are always soft nocturnal exhalations and murmurs, and the broad, shallow wooden stairs invariably creaked. Chloe's door was ajar. Her voice when she called sounded wide awake: 'Robert, is that you? Could you come in for a minute?'

He hesitated in the doorway, for some reason unwilling to fumble for a light switch and illuminate the darkness. Other people's bedrooms are strange and private places, especially at night. Chloe was silent; Robert, seeing nothing, was aware that she was watching him. A moment's unease as he paused, almost wary, waiting for some animal sense of orientation to reassert itself. The shutters were open, however, so that after a few seconds his eyes became accustomed to the different textures of the dark bedroom lit by the faint reflected light of the night sky. He could make out the shape of the bed as a density beneath the pale fluidity of the mosquito net: a solid, enduring, well-worn marriage bed, place of orderly rituals – matings, procreations and deaths; and the figure lying there was what – priestess perhaps, or sacrificial victim? He did not allow this fantasy to break the surface of his mind: the small huddled body was Chloe lying in wakefulness, old and perhaps frightened. Stumbling slightly on the rug, he moved forward into the room.

When she spoke her voice at least was familiar. 'Robert, do you think you could perhaps stay with me a bit tonight? It's a terrible imposition, I know, but if you could bear to stay, even just for a little while . . .'

There did not seem to be a chair anywhere near, so he parted the mosquito net diffidently and sat down at the foot of the bed. He cleared his throat. 'Yes, of course,' he said.

A moment's silence. 'I can't sleep,' she explained, 'too many thoughts . . .'

Robert thought he heard a note of pleading uncharacteristic of the self-possessed daytime Chloe. He nearly asked, 'Shall I go over to the village and fetch Maria?' but instead something made him take her hand: 'Of course I'll stay with you tonight, Chloe,' he said with greater confidence.

Somewhere in the depths of the garden an owl hooted and another replied.

'They're out hunting,' she said. 'I used to watch them in the moonlight with my binoculars. Hunting and killing, but at least the death they mete out is swift and sudden.' Her small hand gripped his.

'What is it?' he asked, feeling clumsy, knowing that something was needed, not knowing what.

'Oh Robert, I know it sounds awfully odd, but do you think, well, do you think you could possibly take off your trousers and lie down beside me for a bit . . . Just your trousers I mean, please don't misunderstand, dreadfully demanding of me – it's only that I think I'd like to feel a man's legs beside me tonight.'

All sorts of mysterious things can happen in the darkness that could never happen by electric light: the darkness is another dimension in which not only bodies but souls may move free and naked. If he had turned on the light it is probable that Robert would have felt excruciatingly embarrassed by this request, would have hesitated, flooded by uncertainties and inadequacies, by old fears of not knowing how to respond; he might even have apologised miserably and turned tail and fled. But in the quiet, velvety, breathing darkness he simply got up, took off his shoes, unbuckled his belt, unzipped his trousers, let them slide to the floor, stepped out of them. As an afterthought, balancing on first one foot then the other, he removed his socks. All these garments he left lying where they fell, as if cast off in heedless passion. He got into bed beside her. She moved closer to him, and they lay in silence side by side. After a few minutes Robert said, 'Wait,' got out of bed again, took off his shirt, took off his underpants. He shivered slightly although the night was warm, got back into bed, turned towards her. She made a little inarticulate sound and rested her head on his shoulder. He slipped his hands under her nightdress and stroked her back, then drew her forwards till she lay half on top of him and very gently encircled her with his arms and legs, clasping her against his body. She felt fragile and warm and somehow precious, like a small bird held in a dream. A faint scent of gardenia emanated from her hair. She sighed, murmured, 'What a very nice person you are, Robert,' then both remained silent. They shifted slightly, settled once more. He found he had a semi-erection; not uncomfortable, of the kind which needed nothing done about it. He listened to her breathing and after a moment realised she was asleep.

Maria had taken to bringing Chloe tea as soon as she arrived in the morning. When she opened the door, carefully balancing the tray against the door jamb as she did so, and found Chloe sitting up in bed in her white nightdress with Robert lying sleeping at her side, apparently naked (here Maria noted and enumerated the trail of clothes strewn on the floor), she simply turned round, closed the door and took the tray back downstairs. Chloe followed her a few minutes later, seated herself at the kitchen table and calmly poured a cup of tea.

Maria clattered pots at the sink for a while, then finally turned and faced her. 'You are far too old for that sort of thing,' she told Chloe sternly, 'it will kill you. It is not normal.'

'It is very normal,' said Chloe, 'and it won't kill me. And anyway' (with a touch of her old spark) 'you have a one-track mind and are rather jumping to conclusions, aren't you.'

'It is not natural.' About this Maria was quite clear and very firm; she never, however, thought quite clearly about why it was that after this episode she felt a new respect for Robert.

Robert himself, waking alone in Chloe's bed, was far less horrified than he would have expected, albeit uncertain of the implications and thus (he admitted to himself) slightly anxious as to what might be required of him. He did not see Chloe at breakfast, did not ask Maria about her as he sometimes did (and indeed did not notice Maria's assessing glance), felt restless as he waited at the gate for the man who was at long last due to deliver the new metal barriers for the irrigation channels. When she appeared at lunch she seemed her usual self, though she ate little; she made no reference to the previous night apart from saying quite simply, 'Thank you, Robert, for your kindness.' In the evening she bade him sleep well and said, 'I shall be quite all right tonight.' He thus retired to his own room, closed the door, and went to bed, although after a moment he got up and opened the door again.

Chloe woke in the night and felt herself to be flooded by such a strange warmth that her immediate reaction was to think, 'I have become senile and incontinent. The humiliations of old age.' However, an instant's investigation showed that this was not the case; as she sat up in bed she realised that the warm wetness was feeling rather than fact, and after a few more seconds that the feeling was located in mind rather than body. Chloe, who never dreamed, had got out of the habit of recognising dreams.

Robert slept dreamlessly.

If there is a crime, she thought, for which one is punished it is the humiliation of another human being. This is a trespassing within the private armoured space of dignity. She was speaking to Robert in her mind: 'It is in any case not easy to maintain one's dignity when caught, naked and vulnerable, more or less *in flagrante delicto*, by an irate and fully clothed husband who stalks through the garden with his rifle like a jealous, punitive Jehovah, yet the ultimate humiliation was the fact that I was not afraid, that I shielded him, that I stepped in front of him, proud and naked and invulnerable. A silence shattered for ever by the cold, hard sound of a rifle being armed: I had no choice, for I understood that Michalis intended to castrate him. Neither of them spoke. The only words were mine, contemptuous, humiliating, so that in the end he turned the rifle on himself and destroyed whatever part of the brain gives people the power to speak their feelings. And for him the ultimate humiliation was that he did not die.'

Robin puts his clothes on hastily, his fingers stiff with shock and horror, fumbling the buttons. Chloe does not bother, runs naked to the house and stands naked in the hall, in front of all the servants, telephoning. The time for pretences seems past.

She does not consider the unwisdom of this, though in fact this shameless nakedness is part of the breaking of taboos that makes more than one man in the neighbourhood later consider the idea of raping her; it is Maria who with unerring instinct protects her by spreading the witch stories.

But this, of course, is in the time to come when Robin has long gone. He leaves as soon as he decently can. He comes to the hospital on his way to catch the ferry and their farewells are said in its tired, dusty garden under the shade of a scrawny acacia; he does not know what to say, cannot quite meet her eyes, in the end in desperation simply kisses her hand. She says, 'Go safely, Robin,' and that is all. Chloe never cries; her eyes are dry and her feelings raw and harsh. She goes inside and stands at the window, looking towards the sea. From this day onwards she feels for scarlet canna lilies a harsh and virulent loathing.

The oldest goddess simply bides her time and drinks whatever spilt blood comes her way.

Robert and Anthony sometimes went swimming on Saturday afternoons; 'The only thing,' Anthony had said, 'is that it means going rather far afield, I'm afraid, since all the beaches near at hand are covered with serried ranks of the most unlovely bodies imaginable, and as for the water, well, one does rather dread to think what goes into it.' When Chloe (with an elaborate politeness that he only later interpreted as defiance) said, 'I have a great desire to go to the sea, Robert – if it is not too much trouble, do you think you would mind perhaps taking me tomorrow morning?' he thus knew exactly where to take her, even before she added, 'What I'd really like would be somewhere lonely.'

'Going to the sea' is one thing, and swimming another. Robert had imagined that Chloe probably wanted to sit on the beach for a while, enjoying the silvery tranquillity of early morning (for he had found her already waiting for him when he got up at six, so they had set out shortly after); hence he was appalled when she calmly began to take off her clothes, with the result that he bellowed at her, 'What the *fuck* do you think you're doing?'

'Getting undressed,' she replied, quite uncowed by this uncharacteristic outburst.

'No,' he said, 'no, Chloe, I can't possibly allow you to go into the water, it's out of the question, I'm sorry, but absolutely no.' He wished he had not thought of such a lonely place to bring her.

'Help me,' she said. By now she was stark naked. 'Listen to me, Robert. It's very simple. I want to immerse myself in the sea. I want you to help me in case I'm not very steady. I don't think a few minutes in the water will kill me. It matters to me. Please help me. It is as undignified for me to beg as it would be for you to restrain me by brute force.'

It was, he later reflected, in part the dignity of her small, pale, almost hairless body and in part the tenderness of that strange night together which made him agree against all normal judgment.

'Not for more than one minute at most, then.'

Robert's swimming things were in the back of the car, yet he said to himself 'Might as well be hung for a sheep as for a lamb' and thus fetched only the towel. He took off his clothes and helped Chloe down to the water's edge; she stumbled slightly on the uneven pebbles and flinched at the early morning coolness of the water, whereupon Robert picked her up and carried her until he was waist-deep in the sea, then set her down and stood behind her with his arms around her. After a moment, in silence, he picked her up again and carried her, unresisting, back to the beach. He dried her as best he could with the towel, then dressed her as one might a small child who obediently raises arm or leg for each garment to be put on. She was shivering. Robert wished he had a jacket or pullover with him; in the absence of any other garment he draped his shirt round her shoulders. He settled her in the car and drove home as fast as possible. She sat facing away from him, so that for a moment he wondered whether she might be crying – apparently not, though, for she was dry-eyed when she finally turned towards him and said, 'I can't tell you about it.'

It is not really possible to explain to anyone about the sea lying in the lap of the earth.

'You don't have to,' he answered, 'it's all right.'

19

Robert never told anyone – not even Annie – about either of these two moments of tender intimacy with Chloe. He did, however, say to Anthony not so long afterwards, 'You were right, very strange things happen when one unbuttons.'

Anthony gave him a close look and asked, 'Do you mean unzipping your flies, Robert, or are you by any chance talking about metaphorical unbuttoning?'

'The second. Both actually.'

This was a week after Chloe's funeral, when Robert had packed his things and moved into Anthony's flat for his last few days before leaving; to his own possessions had been added an old and dented tin trunk containing neat bundles of children's exercise books which Robert had found labelled with his name.

'Are you crying?' Annie had asked when she telephoned on the morning of Chloe's death. (The timing of this call seemed to Robert to be pure, loving telepathy; Annie, who had in fact been intending to tell him that she was two months pregnant, decided that this was the wrong moment and didn't disillusion him.)

'No.' Then, 'Yes, a little. I'd sort of got fond of her.'

Robert, having no experience of village funerals, was taken by surprise when the lid of Chloe's coffin was removed at the graveside. For once, however, he knew instinctively what was needed and thus bent and kissed her small cold hands crossed neatly on her breast, after which the coffin was closed once more and lowered into the ground.

'She wanted to be buried in the garden,' he told Annie after this, 'but I chickened out of saying anything or trying to get permission.'

Annie was amply comforting.

Anthony, too, had hugged him and said, 'Robbie darling, once people are dead it doesn't matter, look at it that way.'

This was what Robert had been saying to himself. Nevertheless, he felt that he had an undischarged debt; thus, after examining the contents of Chloe's cigar box, he telephoned Jeremy in order to find out what a couple of lines of Latin meant, then wrote one of these lines out on a sheet of paper in careful, clearly legible capitals and went to a stone-cutter. Two days later, before moving out, he took Chloe's car for the last time and collected the engraved stone. On an impulse he went into the dining-room and removed the diamond ring from the neck of the decanter. Maria materialised in the doorway. 'I'm not stealing it,' he said defensively as he placed it in the cigar box, then, 'come and see, if you want.' She followed him into the garden, but when she saw the small hole he had dug beneath the cypress tree was quite emphatic that this was not right. She said something that Robert couldn't understand, then impatiently took him by the wrist and led him to the Turkish graves. 'Here,' she said.

And thus it was among the white irises that Robert dug another small grave and buried the box with its apparently random contents: a button, a fifty-lepta coin (once worth half a drachma but now no longer valid currency), a few sheets of paper (three letters and two Latin poems), a postcard of a fossilised winged reptile, a few faded flower petals, a lock of fair hair, a small black pebble, a diamond ring. The stone that he placed on top was a plain slab of limestone bearing the words *Nox est perpetua una dormienda.*

*   *   *

Chloe left her property to the relatively newly founded department of botany of the local university. Much of the outlying land was sold off and the house was subsequently restored but the garden remained unaltered and all the graves untouched.

Robert's daughter was born at the beginning of February, on the feast of Candlemas. She seemed to him to be extraordinarily tiny and frail, though Annie assured him with great pride that she was, on the contrary, rather large as new-born babies go. She had a feathering of straight, silky black hair. Her hands and feet were exquisite. Her name – to which both parents had contributed – was Chloe Valentine.

There be three things which are too wonderful for me, yea, four which I know not: The way of an eagle in the air; the way of a serpent upon a rock, the way of a ship in the midst of the sea; and the way of a man with a maid.

A NOTE ON THE AUTHOR

Born in London, Petrie Harbouri has lived in
Greece since 1970. She has worked as a
translator of Greek fiction into English. Her first novel
Graffiti is published by Bloomsbury.

A NOTE ON THE TYPE

The text of this book is set in Linotype Sabon, named after the type founder, Jacques Sabon. It was designed by Jan Tschichold and jointly developed by Linotype, Monotype and Stempel, in response to a need for a typeface to be available in identical form for mechanical hot-metal composition and hand composition using foundry type.

Tschichold based his design for sabon roman on a fount engraved by Garamond, and sabon italic on a fount by Granjon. It was first used in 1966 and has proved an enduring modern classic.